Rich Highness

Sam Earsman

Contents

1. ♛ That big project that almost end my school life 1
2. ♛ I started a fight in a cafe. Bad idea, by the way! 11
3. ♛ Heir of the Skyler Group 22
4. ♛ The boy who cared for me 33
5. ♛ Revealing his identity to the whole world 39
6. ♛ The truth that cursed his life 49
7. ♛ My replay of Titanic 58
8. ♛ You drive me crazy 66
9. ♛ Little Talks with myself 73
10. ♛ Our love that is bleeding 80
11. ♛ Say something 89
12. ♛ Announcements of new book in the "Simplicity Series" 99

That big project that almost end my school life

You're back with TalkMusic. Before we get to our next song, how are you today? It's the first day of winter, and the road is getting thicker with snow. To commemorate the upcoming Christmas season, TalkMusic presents "All I Want For Christmas" by Mariah Carey!

I turned on the radio as Dad drove his shiny black Audi. Looking at the window, I saw snow falling from the misty white sky into the ground, melting completely as it reached the surface of earth. Dad was forcing his eyes to see through the haze in front of us. Two cups of hot chocolate separated us, and I licked my lip as I took my cup.

While Dad was panicking in his drive-my-daughter-to-school world, I was enjoying my time in the brown-chocolate world. Cold wind brushed down my face, and I quickly brought my hot cup closer to me, trying to pass the warmth to my face.

Crossing my arms, I tightened my grip on my thick orange coat for more warmth. With my legs intertwined, I rubbed my cold gloved hands on my black stocking and gritted my teeth as I realized what I was wearing. Dad glanced at me and chuckled.

"I told you not to wear skirts," Dad said, his eyes focused back on the road.

"I didn't know it would be this cold!" I argued. "It was all warm yesterday. I didn't expect it to be freezing Antarctica the next day."

Dad moved forward from his seat, his seatbelt tugging him to lean back, but he didn't listen as he narrowed his eyes, trying to see clearer. His eyes scanned forcefully through the fog like an x-ray machine. "Girls these days and their fashion," he groaned as he made a sharp left turn.

I gave him the don't-you-dare look, but he didn't catch my eye. "Dads and their old fashioned clothing," I argued back, bringing my hot chocolate to his nose.

He was about to sip my drink when I pulled it back away from him, laughing. I drank the whole chocolate drink as Dad stared at me with disbelief, misery in his eyes. Still freezing to death, I took his chocolate drink and took a sip. Dad's jaw dropped, and he gave me the puppy-dog eyes.

"It taste so good, Dad. I wish you can taste it, but it won't be enough for both of us," I teased.

Dad muttered something unintelligible, but I couldn't hear him through TalkMusic, playing Mariah Carey's song. Like a cue, Dad wore his earmuffs and flinched when he heard my voice piercing through his protection.

"I don't want a lot for Christmas!" I began singing. Dad reached out his hand to turn off the radio, but I quickly slapped him off. "There is just one thing I need," I continued the lyrics, pulling Dad's business tie.

"You and your horrible—"

I pinched him, and he quickly changed his words. "—your beautiful voice," he ended before glaring at me.

When he saw my school gates, Dad looked more that relieved. A huge glassed building welcomed our car, followed by many other high classed vehicles starting from cars to long limos.

"See you, Dad!" I kissed him in the cheek before exiting the car. I quickly regretted the action when a gust of freezing cold wind hit my skin. The coldness didn't freeze my nerve, but it made me run like an athlete to the nearest warm building.

When warmness started to settle into my body, I sighed gratefully before turning around to find my locker. I wasn't new here, but after a few weeks of holiday, I could see the little differences from the last season decoration.

The school's hallway was painted white. A small snowman replica stood at the end of each hallway. When I looked up, I saw the newly painted white ceiling with cotton attached to make it look like now. I noticed some bubble machines hidden in small corners to make fake snowflakes. Then I recognized the way to my locker.

Time to become Santa, I thought to myself. When I got to my locker, it was crowded by every of my classmates. They saw me coming and started to squeal when I showed a huge red bag of presents in my hand. My heart bloomed as they ran to surround me.

"Constanza!" I felt someone hug me from behind, squeezing me tightly.

I coughed. "Ra—Rachel—can't—breathe—"

Rachel, my best friend, released me. "Oh, sorry," she said. She stared at the huge crowd building up around my locker and gasped. "You're becoming Santa again this year?" she questioned.

I nodded, holding out the huge red bag I had since the morning.

Then heaven became real. I started giving presents. A month ago, I made my whole class write what they wanted for Christmas on a slip of paper. Of course, I told them it must be under 100 dollars. I wouldn't want to spend my whole saving account for my Santa project every year.

"A makeup collection?" Rachel stared at me with disbelief. "This is so amazing!" She hugged me one more time. "You're the best of the best of the best of the best of the—"

I grinned. "I know. I am that awesome."

My classmates were still crowding in front of me, pushing each other to get to the front. Quickly, I started taking the presents one by one and calling each names. Each person hugged me before they open their presents with their group of friends, and each person left me their smiles and gratitude. That every little smile and sounds of gratitude inspired me to become Santa. I love giving.

Giving all the presents away, I felt my arms getting tired, and when the last person took his present, I brushed the small beads of sweat on my forehead. It was finally done. My time to become the school's Santa was done, and I would have to wait for another year to feel the same happiness.

"Hey, you have one more present left," Rachel said.

I rummaged through the red bag and found the last present covered in red candy cane paper wrappings. There was a card on top, and the words Aiden Skyler were written neatly on the small snowman card.

"Are you planning to give it to him?" Rachel asked. They all knew Aiden rarely went to school. My prediction is he was trying to avoid people. He wasn't here every day for that specific reason, but other than my hypothesis, no one really knows why.

"I don't know, Rachel. I'll give it to him when I meet him today," I told her.

Then the school bell rang, indicating the start of school.

My first class was anthropology. Sometimes I wondered why the school had this subject. I realized that this school is a prestigious school with high standards, but the subject was thoroughly useless. When I entered the classroom, I met Mr. Rene's glare before sitting at the last row.

"Good morning class," Mr. Rene said. Then he started discussing about the semester's introductory topic: human behavior. As he started spitting out words from the dictionary, I zoned out. The present for Aiden Skyler was still inside my bag, and it grew heavier as I mixed it together with my textbooks.

You're afraid of that outcast, Constanza?

But Aiden Skyler wasn't like your typical outcast. He was the notorious outcast, having the personalities of a jerk, a bad boy. All the girls would kiss his steps, but he wasn't that jerk who wanted attention. He was the jerk who wanted people away from him. My thoughts were mainly focused on him when the door barged open.

The whole class woke up from their sleep and stared at the door. There on the door, Aiden Skyler made his appearance to class. With dark circles surrounding his beautiful blue eyes, he ran a hand through his tousled black hair before glaring at Mr. Rene.

"Excuse me?" Mr. Rene said, disappointed in his lateness. "I thought I made it clear that I don't want you late in my classes. You're already failing."

His bad boy personality flipped Mr. Rene. Aiden ignored him and walked toward the back seat. When his gorgeous blue eyes met my chocolate ones, I froze in place. It wasn't my first time to make eye contact with him, but it was my first time to see his eyes looking so innocent, not the usual mischievous glint.

"Is anyone sitting here?" he asked, gesturing to the seat beside me.

I began to stutter in his presence, his powerful aura confusing my head. "U—uh, I—I don't t—think—"

"I take that as a no," he said, giving me a lazy smirk before sitting down next to me. I stared at him as he rested his head on the soft wooden table before he dozed off to sleep. Mr. Rene noticed him sleeping next to me but let it slipped. He was used to Aiden sleeping in his class every week.

After a few notes and class discussion, the whole class was complaining on how boring and useless Mr. Rene's class was.

"We're going to have a project!" Mr. Rene said in delight, eying us with the this- is-what-you-get-for-hating-my-subject look.

The class, who was still focused on something else, turned back their attention to our teacher with a groan. "No fair!" a student said.

Mr. Rene gave the typical teachers evil smile. "It'll be great! Best of all, I'm going to use my favorite method to put you all in groups of two!"

I gulped, knowing where he was going to.

"I will pick your partners," Mr. Rene, our teacher, declared, "in alphabetical order."

I swallowed, knowing my partner, and silently hoping for Mr. Rene to change his mind and let us pick our own partner.

He took his attendance list from his teacher's table and began assigning the class in partners.

"Aiden Skyler and Constanza Adeline," he said.

I whined loudly, but Aiden didn't stir. The whole class turned around, sharing their sympathy with me.

Yes, it's him and me again.

"I'll give you time today to talk to your partners about your project for the rest of the period," Mr. Rene added, adding misery to my already horrible fate.

I raised my hand. Mr. Rene glanced at me, and I gestured to the sleeping Aiden who was mumbling something in his sleep. "What should I do to him?" I asked.

Mr. Rene gave me an approving look. "Go wake him up."

I gulped. Moving my seat closer to his, I felt my movements getting slower, together with the world that seemed to be spinning slower than usual. I saw Aiden sleeping peacefully on his table, his beautiful eyes shut. Thousands of girls would pay just to see his eyes open, but that wouldn't work. Aiden hated attention.

When Mr. Rene called a representative of each group to get the project prompts, I exhaled, finally finding a reason to get away from Aiden. I received the prompt and thanked Mr. Rene, but my smile quickly dropped from my face when I read the project title written in bold.

Name: The Love Project

Questions to find out:

-How is love created?

-Why is it created?

-What are the feelings of love?

-Why do people love?

Discuss these questions with your partner, and come with a 2000 word essay on your topic. Each group will receive different topics, so don't bother to cheat. It's due in 10 days.

Sincerely,

Mr. Rene

The whole class began to whisper when they read their prompts, and complains started filling the air, making me sick. I got back to my seat and placed the prompt on Aiden's table, somewhere far away from his head. Beside his head, I saw a black leathered agenda.

Curious, I took it in my hand and opened it. His writing impressed me. It was neat, not like any other boys' scribbling. Inside, he wrote: meeting grandfather, Radio Station employment, meeting with hotel management.

I was about to flip to the next page when a hand appeared between the pages and harshly grabbed the book from me.

"Hey!" I tried to forcefully grab the notebook back, but he took it from me before giving me a furious look.

"Do. Not. Touch. Other. People's. Things," Aiden said, putting his small book inside the pocket of his leather jacket before adding, "Without. Permission."

I gulped and looked at him sheepishly, feeling my cheeks blooming red. "I'm sorry," I confessed. "Scholarly curiosity."

He shook his head, giving the look of disapproval. "Now what are you doing in my table?"

"U—uh," I stuttered. "P—project." I gave him the prompt, and he frowned as his eyes scanned the title.

"A love project?" he asked me, furrowing his forehead.

I nodded. "Yes."

"Fine," he announced. "So when are we going to work on this? I'm really busy you know." He chuckled and gave me a smile, that smile that almost made me faint with a heart attack.

With my words stuck in my throat, I gagged and made funny noises. By then, the whole class was staring at both of us, and some of the girls gave me funny looks like what are you doing? Impress him already! and what the heck, girl.

Suddenly, Aiden's hand was on my face. I tried to hide my blush so badly, but I knew he'd caught it.

"Do I intimidate you?" he asked, a bit of concern in his voice.

I tried to shake my head, but I was frozen, his hand still on my face. "I—I—"

Then he took his hand off my face and scribbled something on a piece of paper (that came from absolutely nowhere). I was almost relieved that he looked away when he turned back at me and gave me the paper. I grimaced at it before asking, "What's this?"

"There's my number and the address to TalkMusic Radio Station. Meet me there today at 5, and we'll discuss this project. I hope we can finish it quickly," he quickly speeded.

Before I could say a thing, the bell rang, and he exited quickly before anyone does.

♛ I started a fight in a cafe. Bad idea, by the way!

By the time the bell rang, indicating lunch time, everyone inside the school area had figured out the project incident, and to be precise, about me and Aiden. My body shuddered as I thought of him working together with me. We might as well burn the whole city just for a simple agreement on using color pencils or markers.

"We're like heaven and hell!" I screamed with disgust. "He's so ugly and disgusting! Why am I so kind to him? Why do I feel different around him?"

Rachel rolled her eyes. "Duh, because he's actually really hot and smart, everything unlike you and your small brain?"

I gave her my glare before stomping into the cafeteria. Once I pushed the glassed double doors, a huge glassy place greeted me. The cafeteria at school was like a greenhouse. Tall trees and flowers filled the area, and many small tables were scattered around the place. High quality food made by the best chefs around the world resided here.

A smile would usually crawl up my face every time I see the beautiful cafeteria, but with the stares of everyone around now, I felt like curling into a ball, somewhere in the corner of this world.

My eardrum were almost deafening when I heard every single person in the cafeteria whispered about the trendiest gossip.

That's her: Constanza Adeline, Aiden's partner.

She's so damn lucky.

I look better than her. Aiden would like me better than her.

I clenched my hands into fists as passed the popular girls' seat beside the hot guys. Some of the guys winked at me, and I gave them my usual smile before sitting at my usual place.

Rachel quickly rushed towards me, trying to catch up. "Geez," she said, "don't be too sensitive!"

"I'm not," I muttered. "I'm just annoyed."

She blinked. "No offence, Stanza, that's the same thing. You're being too pessimistic about the whole idea."

"He's a poor useless kid, Rachel," I argued, every of my words laced with venom. "I heard he pays his school bills late for the third time this year."

Rachel frowned. "He might have his own reasons."

"Doesn't everything click inside your head?" I asked, furious. "He pays everything late. He's an outcast. I heard he works in a radio station, maybe as a cleaning janitor. He's definitely the definition of poor guy."

"If you don't want to be one group with him, you couldn't just ask Mr. Rene to exchange you with me," Rachel suggested. "I'll be fine with him."

The thought of him and me being in different groups gave me the electricity. I wanted it more than ever, but another feeling flowed through me. It felt like losing someone important to you.

Since when has he become that important? I thought. Through gritted teeth, I tried to clear his name from my head, but the effort was thoroughly useless. Every time I tried to delete him from my dictionary, I would always see his name, still there with more definitions under his name.

Aiden Skyler (noun): 1. Jerk. 2. Lovely 3. Outcast 4. Beautiful 5. Might be poor 6. My heart.

I shook my head and came back to the reality. Rachel was staring at me with intense eyes, and she grinned at me. "You like him, don't you?" Rachel taunted, grinning like an idiot.

My cheeks flooded with redness, and I turned my head to look at the sunflowers beside our seats. "These flowers are so beautiful!" I said with delight, trying to avoid her conversation.

Rachel grabbed my jaw and turned my attention back to her. She gave me the evil eyes and smirked. "I knew it," she declared. "You're so red I might mistake you for a huge tomato."

"No, I don't like him!" I battled. "You know nothing about me, and—"

"And you don't know anything about me that allows you to talk about me behind my back." I felt something run through my skin, something that sent trepidation through my nerves. When I turned around, a pair of bright blue eyes threw daggers at me. My teeth started to chatter when I felt his hand squeezed my shoulder. I was frozen when he brought his face closer to me.

"I—I—"I started.

"Please don't hurt my friend!" Rachel begged. She was almost on her knees when Aiden chuckled, pulling himself away from me. I exhaled when his hand was off my shoulder.

"You act like I'm a murderer," he said, chuckling.

"So you're not?" Rachel halfwhispered.

He looked offended. "Do I look like one?"

"Yeah, he looks more like a janitor to me," I added.

He glared at me, and Rachel mentioned, "Hot janitor."

"What are you doing here, Mr. Know it All Aiden?" I questioned.

He raised his hands. "You don't have to be that hostile. I'm a good boy here."

I rolled my eyes, definitely not convinced. "You don't look like your self-proclaimed good boy."

"I'm just making sure you come after school to the radio station. My schedule is busy, and I don't have time for stupid school projects." His usual arrogant voice was back, and my anger boiled again.

"I am coming," I said through clenched teeth. "But I'll make sure your busy schedule is ruined."

He raised an eyebrow. "Your point?"

"I'm making your world into hell," I pointed out.

"You dare?"

Somehow, I was hesitating. This was THE Aiden Skyler, the most handsome outcast in the whole world. His presence gave the Aiden-Knows-It-All aura.

Are you sure?

"Yes," I clarified. "I dare."

He smiled. "I'll see you after school then. I'm looking forward to your dare."

I asked Rachel to take me to TalkMusic after school. She stopped her black Audi in front of the station, but after getting looks from the local people, she decided to leave me with Aiden, all alone and helpless.

"You're on your own, Stanza. Sorry!" she screamed before speeding off with her brand new car and with me sighing on the sidewalk.

The TalkMusic building appeared in front of me. White creamy walls with the aroma of coffee surrounded the receptionist room. A woman behind the receptionist table greeted me.

"Excuse me," I said. "I'm looking for some janitor guy named Aiden Skyler."

The woman furrowed her forehead, confused. "A janitor? Aiden Skyler?"

I gulped. "What's wrong with Aiden Skyler?"

"There's no janitor named Aiden Skyler here."

"Then, is there anyone named Aiden Skyler in this building?" I asked impatiently.

The woman stared at me blankly. Surprise and confusion were clearly noted on her face. Her forehead seemed to scream what the heck. Without saying anything, I walked toward the small arrangement of sofas at the edge of the room, beside a small cafe.

I searched for Aiden's note inside my bag. When I saw his number scribbled on the paper, I quickly pressed the buttons of my cell phone to call him. The matter was: Aiden was the worst jerk ever.

"The number you are calling is unreachable," the operator chimed in after several beeps. "Call back again a few minutes later."

Silently, I cursed before furiously punching the numbers on my phone to call again. The same operator woman answered my phone call, and after several calls, I was literally throwing and jumping on my cell phone

"The number you are calling is unreachable," I mimicked, my tone full of poison.

"Excuse me?"

I turned around to find the receptionist woman looking at me, her eyes showing the are-you-an-idiot expression. Tired, I grabbed my phone that was lying on the floor, broken, before sitting back down on the sofa. "What?" I asked.

"I found the Aiden Skyler you're looking for. There's approximately around three Aidens around here. Well, none of them are janitors. They're actually our staffs," the receptionist woman said on and on.

I nodded. "Thank you."

"Yeah, you should be." Aiden appeared out of nowhere. He was wearing a black suit over his white shirt and jeans. When he stood beside the receptionist, the woman actually blushed before retreating to her desk behind the receptionist counter.

I pointed at the time on my cell phone. "You're late," I pointed out.

"I said after school, not specifically when," he said. "And one call is enough you know. You don't have to call me for ten times. It gets really annoying."

"It actually took me ten calls to get you down here." I grimaced before crossing my arms.

He sighed before gesturing me to the cafe behind the sofas. "You remember the project? Let's do it now. I'm really busy," he muttered.

I grabbed my bag from the sofa and entered the cafe with Aiden. He gave a polite nod to the receptionist woman before following my steps. The aroma of coffee and tea welcomed me into the cafe.

Picking a sofa at the edge of the cafe, I threw my bag towards the sofa before running to the cashier. Apparently, the so-not gentleman slipped in front of me and asked for his order.

"Hey! I was here first," I complained.

Aiden looked back and stared at me before giving the cashier guy his money. "What do you want?" he asked.

I was taken aback. "You're paying for me?"

He rolled his eyes. "For your information, I'm not that poor. They're all rumors."

I pretended to scuff something under my shoes on the ground. "Uh, vanilla latte, please?" I asked politely.

"And one vanilla latte," Aiden added to the cashier guy. The guy nodded and told us that our orders would be delivered to our tables. I nodded, and then, we sat down on the sofa. Aiden was seated in front of me. He stared at me with his blue eyes and a smile on his lips.

"What?" I asked. "Is there something on my face?"

He laughed. "No, you're just weird."

"Thanks," I muttered. "Now, let's start the project." I took my laptop from my purple bag. For your information, I stuffed many things inside my bag that is necessary for survival and enjoyment. Laptops are essential in our daily lives, so I categorized it in the "survival" category.

"How are we going to make this?" I asked. "Mr. Rene told us to make an essay, so I think we should do a little research. You know, we should also add a bit of science into—"

I went on and on. Aiden kept on staring. My voice was getting louder and louder, my hands also moving. "Hello?" I asked. "Are you listening?"

Aiden blinked. "I'm sorry. What?"

I glared at him. "Are you taking this as a joke?"

"What?"

"This is a project!" I shouted just when the cashier guy placed our drinks on the table. When he heard my disagreement, he jumped and quickly excused himself.

"I know, I know," Aiden reasoned. "Relax. So, yeah, research?" He was definitely unfocused.

My eyes scanned the room for anything that can smash Aiden's hard head, but the whole cafe was only filled with other benches and tables. Then my eyes landed on our coffee. An idea was processed inside my head, and I grinned evilly as I took my vanilla latte.

"Aiden?" I asked sweetly and deceivingly.

Aiden looked up, and just as his eyes drilled through mines, I spilled my hot vanilla late on his suit and shirt.

"Holy—"Aiden quickly grabbed a tissue and cringed as the hotness seeped into his skin. He was literally cussing all the way when he saw his own hot drink still on the table. Suddenly, his hands grabbed his drink, but before he could throw it, my instincts clicked in.

I jumped and hid behind my sofa. When I heard the splash of his coffee hit my sofa and his cursing, I grinned mischievously.

"Constanza Adeline!" Aiden screamed and launched empty cups on top of my head.

"Hey!" I retorted.

Then everything turned chaotic. We were throwing things at each other, anything soft and harmless. The cashier guy was trying to separate us, but the matter was: we didn't want to be separated. We were actually having fun on our own. I felt my own smile crawling on my face as I threw a cake from the counter on Aiden's face.

Aiden grabbed the extra cups near the cashier and threw it at me. He laughed when one of the cups hung on my ear. Annoyed, I took the cup and filled it with some water before spraying him with it. Soon, I saw Aiden with some warm cup of water.

I giggled as I ran swiftly around the coffee tables, making a complete mess. From somewhere, I heard the cashier guy screaming at the telephone. "Are we in trouble?" I asked Aiden in a sudden.

He blinked back to realization and looked around. Most tables and chairs were flipped up-side down, and our sofa was smeared with lots of coffee stains. Empty paper cups were scattered everywhere, and the sign of a food fight was evident with the stains of cream on the walls.

As if my question was a cue, I saw someone tall dressed like a police coming towards us. “Damn it!” I cursed, and Aiden took that chance to wipe his creamy hands on my shirt.

“Aiden!” I screamed, but the police was already behind him, cuffing both his wrists.

He glared at me. “You have your ways to ruin my schedule. Remind me to never make dares with you.”

Another police officer came out of nowhere and grabbed me. My hands were pulled behind me, and the cuffs clicked, indicating that it was locked.

“You’re welcome!” I told Aiden.

Those were my last two words before something else went wrong. The cashier guy who looked so red and angry was holding a baton in his hand.

“You son of a—“

Aiden turned his head towards the cashier guy, wanting to apologize. His mouth formed the word sorry, but the baton was already on its way. With a loud sound, almost like a crack, the baton landed on Aiden’s head.

The police was taken aback, and he quickly grabbed the cashier guy before he could run away. I stared in disbelief as Aiden’s head lolled, a scream of pure agony escaping from his lips. His face twisted with severe pain, and he fell, his body hitting the ground with a thud before his eyes rolled to the back of his head.

♛ Heir of the Skyler Group

"Are you okay?"

Those were the first three words that I threw out of my mouth after the accident. Inside the holding room, I sat on the cold metal chair and rested my hands on the table. There were two cups of cold water on the table, but after the whole circumstances that just happened, Aiden and I didn't have the energy or the willingness to do anything. We stared at the walls, quietness filling the space between us.

My heart was racing. I remembered blood pouring out of Aiden's head. It wasn't that bad though. It took them a few minutes to bandage his head and make him drink some medicines. Despite his unconsciousness, Aiden was quickly awake. In fact, he had opened his eyes after an hour travelling inside the police's car. Apparently, the bad traffic just slowed down our imminent interrogation in the police station.

The police tried to convince Aiden to go see the doctor, but he kindly refused. He told them that he was feeling fine, but I wondered if that was really the truth. Throughout the whole way to the police station, I saw him looking out through the windows, examining every single snow that started to fall. He looked out with sad eyes. I've never seen him that sad. Maybe it's because I wasn't always there around him.

Now that he was my project partner, I got to know his real feelings. And yeah, he was kind of pathetic. His strong cool boy appearance disappeared now. When he caught be looking at him, he gave me a reassuring smile. Aiden the bad boy had just smiled to me inside a bloody police car. And then, I decided to assume that Aiden was literally insane.

Now, right across of me, Aiden rested his head on the cold table and winced as he tried to turn his head. I flinched when he twisted in pain. The bandages that circled his head were turning red again. Blood soaked parts of his bandages, and by the looks of his tired eyes, Aiden was trying to stay awake. His head turned out to be worst that it looked. Somehow, when we were fighting inside the cafe, he bumped something. It causes an external bleeding on the surface of his head, and the symptoms of nausea started coming up on him. So now, not only that some cafe dude just hit his head with a baton, he accidentally hits his head somewhere.

"I'm fine," he said in a sound that was barely a whisper. When he really turned his head, I saw his dry lips cracked. Aiden looked at the cups of cold water on the table. His hand started to grab the cup, but then the pain screamed inside his head again. He curled his hands into fists.

I hastily grabbed the cup and pressed it against his lips. "Drink," I told him. He obeyed. I held the cup as he drank the entire cup, leaving no drops of water leaking to the table. When he shook his head, I pulled the cup away and threw it to the corner of the room. I looked at the other fully filled cup of water resting near my portion of the table.

My throat was burning, but when I glanced back at Aiden, I couldn't drink it anymore.

"Do you want more?" I asked, raising the cup.

He shook his head and rested his head back on the surface of the table. Shutting his eyes, he fell asleep with me staring in front of him. For some reason, Aiden just love sleeping. No wonder he slept everywhere: school, shops, and now here. I thought he was just tired. The fact that he could sleep calmly in this situation is totally abnormal. He slept here.

Here.

I gulped. What would Mom do when you got the call from the police? I tried to imagine the situation in my head. How would Mom react? Would she cut me like chicken and boil me for soup?

"What?" Mom shrieked.

"You daughter was arrested—"

Mom closed the phone and grabbed her pouch. "Constanza! I'll definitely kill her, make her into soup, and eat her for dinner."

I shivered at my ridiculous thought. It was funny, but the coldness from my surrounding gave me the nerves. I was afraid. For the first time in my life, I was sitting here in the police station, looking worried. Unlike me, Aiden was asleep soundlessly.

He never cares.

After a few minutes of quietness, the door burst opened. Aiden quickly opened his eyes in surprise and stirred his head towards the door. In front of us, the police officer beamed at us. He raised an eyebrow and mouthed you guys are lucky. Mom quickly emerged into the picture, and my heart melted.

"Hi, Mom," I said, waving my hand.

Mom gave me the most sadistic look in the world. When she batted her thick eyelashes, I quickly sat up straighter. She gave the most menacing look. Aiden's angry eyes were nothing compared to hers. Although Mom was only going to the police station, she wore thick red lipstick as if she wanted to go and seduce someone in the police station.

"Let's go. Hurry, this place gives me the creeps," Mom said out loud.

The police beside her gave her the look.

"Mom!" I retorted. "At least talk about people behind their backs, not directly in front of them!"

The police glared at me.

She glanced blankly. "What?"

My Mom never changed. Her real personality was showing up. That sadistic look was clearly wiped from her face, replaced by a happy cheerful face, when the police decided to leave us alone. She gave me a smile before running on her heels to hug me. "You've finally n!" Mom said delightfully. "You finally got into some trouble ıd acted like an adult! I'm so—"

"Wait," I stopped her. "So you're not angry?"

Mom looked at me with blank eyes. "You actually bought that act? I do have beautiful acting skills."

"Fine, let's go," I said. Just then, I remembered Aiden was still there. He looked at Mom and me as if he was watching a comedy show. There was a hint of a smile on his face, but his eyes mirrored a sad reflection. My heart leaped when I saw more blood leaking into his bandages.

"I'll see you later," he croaked. He was about to fall back asleep, but Mom shook him gently.

"You're coming with us," she said.

Aiden stared at her. "Me? Are you sure?"

Mom nodded. "After all, it was Stanza's fault that you got caught into this."

I groaned. "Mom!"

Aiden chuckled. "She has her ways to make me annoyed, madam."

"Someone finally agreed with me on how annoying you are!" Mom exclaimed, pointing at me.

"You're acting childish, Mom," I warned.

"Oh." Mom brushed her hands against her clothes before walking towards the exit door. "Let's go now. And Stanza, help your boyfriend. He looks like he's struggling."

I flushed faintly. "Mom, he's not my—"

"Come here, and help me, trouble maker," Aiden said.

I glanced back at him and found a smirking Aiden with his billion dollar smile. He looked at me genuinely before getting on his feet. The dizziness quickly took over, and he almost stumbled if I didn't catch him.

"Hah, it's usually the boys who help the girls. Now, it's the other way around. I'm completely pathetic," he muttered. He circled one hand around me. Adjusting himself on me for support, we walked out of the holding room, our breaths heavy after such an experience.

The feeling of going out was beautiful, but when the cold air hit our skin, I recoiled. Aiden almost fell when I lost my balance and decided to release my grip on him.

"Hey!" Aiden exclaimed. I quickly helped him again.

"You're such a baby," I teased.

He rolled his eyes. "You just ruined my whole schedule, and now you're teasing me. Way to go to fix the whole thing."

I darkened. "Sorry, geez, you don't have to be so dense."

Mom honked the car. "Kids, please don't go all romantic in front of me. Get in the car before I leave you two!"

We both quickly rushed inside, and then, Mom drove the way home.

"So, where do you live?"

Since we got inside the car, Mom was bombarding Aiden with lots of questions despite his dizziness. Her questions sounded annoying, but Aiden gave no hints of annoyance. He was already in his best manner and words in front of mom. Heck, he even called her madam.

, I thought the world would end. Since when did the Aiden /ler become this polite?

"I live behind TalkMusic radio station, ma'am," he said.

"Behind that radio station? Whoa, we actually live around there too. Your family must be privileged. I heard from people that you were actually—"Mom searched for the appropriate word—"low in funds."

Aiden coughed. "Those are just rumors, ma'am."

"I heard you can't even buy lunch," Mom pressed.

"Mom, I think you're hurting his pride!" I told her.

"That's not helping, Stanza," he said, chuckling. I gulped when he said my name. Was that the first time he said my name? When was the last time he called my name?

"I actually have enough for lunch," Aiden explained. "But I prefer bringing my own food from home. It tastes better than the food at school."

I gaped at him. "That doesn't make sense at all! The school has one of the best foods in town!"

"Maybe I found this special place with the perfect recipe to make food better than the school?" he suggested.

I muttered something under my breath. "Mr. Know it all, you think you know it all," I muttered.

"You just plagiarized Kelly Clarkson's song," Aiden mentioned.

"You actually listen to music? Wow, that's new," I said, uninterested.

"I work in TalkMusic." He shrugged. "I know a lot about music."

"Can you play the instruments?"

"I play the piano and the violin."

Mom smiled. "You should play for us sometimes. I tried to force Stanza to join that piano course, but she threatened me to hide all my makeup products. She's such an incorrigible girl."

Aiden grinned, and I reddened in embarrassment.

"Sure," Aiden said. "I love playing music. My mom always told me—"

He stopped.

"Yeah?" Mom asked.

He looked aside as if he was trying to hide his face. From the periphery of my eyes, I caught one glance. I saw his eyes before he turned his head. Those eyes were filled with misery. "Nothing," he said.

"What's your name again? I heard those rumors from school. Your name is R—Ryan? Ryder? Ruflo? Pluto? Alladin?" Mom remarked.

"Uh, his name isn't in any of them, Mom," I said.

By then, we were parked in front of my house. Aiden glanced at the huge grey mansion that stood in front of us. Tall pillars surrounded the entrance like the Greek architecture. My eyes brightened when I got out of the car and quickly headed for shelter from the pouring snow.

"Impressed?" I asked when Aiden came by my side below the shelter.

He shook his head. "This is barely half of my house."

I rolled my eyes. "Liar."

"So why am I here?" he asked Mom.

"You're staying for a night! You can call your parents inside. The snow is thick, so I don't think anyone can pick you up. Don't worry. Our house has everything. You can use one of Stanza's dad's shirts, and—"

"Mom, he got the main idea," I said.

"Fine."

Aiden looked around. When we stepped inside the house, his eyes looked surprised. My house was lined with many paintings that could cost thousands of dollars each. There are vases and other crystal decoration that can easily captivate anyone. Mom was one of the reason why our house was clean, neat, and fully of beautiful decorations. Although she worked with Dad, she always had time for decorations.

"This is impressive," Aiden said.

"Envy my house?"

"Nope," he said, popping the 'p'. "I think you'll be more impressed with my house."

"What's inside your house?" I asked.

"Lots and lots of food."

I glared at him. "Not funny."

Before we knew it, we were walking towards the main room. From the corner of my eyes, I saw Dad and his client talking loudly. There was a contract on the wooden table. The fireplace was lighted, giving warmth to the whole room. The coldness from my skin was taken away, replaced by inevitable warmth. Aiden looked comfortable too, but when he looked at Dad and his client, he looked a little bit uneasy.

"They're talking about something important," he said all of a sudden. "Let's leave. We shouldn't interrupt them." He was clearly trying to avoid them.

Why?

I was about to climb the stairs to my room when Dad called us.

"Stanza?"

"Hi, Dad," I beamed, turning back at Dad and his client.

"Who's with you?" Dad asked.

Aiden turned his head reluctantly and nodded at Dad. "Um, hello, sir," he said.

Then, there was silence. There was no sign from Dad that we could leave. Dad and his client looked at us with widening eyes. No, they weren't looking at us. They were looking at Aiden.

"Is there something wrong with me?" he asked. "Sorry, but—"

The client stood from his seat. "Are you Aiden Skyler?"

How did that client know Aiden?

"Yes, sir," Aiden said. "Do I know you?"

The client gave a forced smile. "You have a meeting with our company a few hours ago. Did you forget to attend?"

Aiden stared. After a few seconds, everything seemed to click for him. "Mr. Kennedy," he said. He walked towards the main room where Dad and his client stood. Shaking Mr. Kennedy's hand, Aiden bowed his head.

"Please forgive my absent. I was having—"he hesitated—"issues," he said.

I looked at Dad and gave him a confused look.

"Mr. Kennedy?" Dad asked, looking at Aiden. "Who is he?"

Mr. Kennedy gave Dad an incredulous look. "You don't know him? He's Aiden Skyler, the youngest CEO in history and heir to all Skyler Group companies. That involves the ownership of TalkMusic, Stanza's school, the malls around, the gasoline stations, the—"

"Aiden Skyler?" Dad screamed the word Skyler.

Aiden gulped. "Uh, yes sir."

Dad examined Aiden with this belief. How could a teenager like him be a freaking CEO?

Aiden smiled awkwardly as everyone looked at him with wonders.

And the rumors of Aiden being the poorest kid in school had just ended.

He had just reigned supreme among all of us.

He was the CEO of everything. The Skyler Group owned half all the companies in the country.

The boy who cared for me

His Rich Highness

Chapter 4- The Boy Who Cared For Me

Breaking the awkward silence, Aiden excused himself from the main room. "I'm sorry for disturbing your business," he said politely. When none of the parties said a word, he added, "So if you'll excuse me..."

Dad didn't even blink as Aiden walked away. His eyes were glued on Aiden's back. Maybe he was wondering how a young boy like Aiden could be one of the most powerful people in the whole country. Maybe Dad and I were having the same thought.

Bullshit.

Am I dreaming?

All the rumors of Aiden at school couldn't be a total lie. His rumor had grown through the years. The whole town had known this rumor. Aiden was that poor kid, the guy who barely cared about a single thing in the world. He was the most charming and daring person the school ever known. Nothing fears him. He reigns supreme upon other teenage creatures in the world.

I looked behind me. Aiden was following me up the stairs to my room. He forced his head down. Slowly, I could feel his mood. It was difficult and messed up. He looked stressed out, like he might burn the house any sooner to satisfy his stress.

He can buy anything, Stanza. He's not a poor kid. For goodness sake, he's a multibillionaire that owned every—

"Can you stop that?" Aiden said, his voice stern.

I turned to him in the middle of the stairs and folded my arms. "Stop what?"

He smiled weakly. "You're spelling out every single thought. First, you're not dreaming. This isn't a bullshit dream." He raised both his hands. "This is the real me, the real Aiden."

"I don't care."

"You look disappointed," he remarked.

My feelings had outreached disappointment. Not that I didn't want Aiden to be successful, but I hate being lied to. I wanted everyone to be happy. Trust me, I'm not that mean person. But I hate liars. Why should he lie anyway? Maybe he wanted to show off his extreme power once his real identity was torn down. Yeah, Aiden was that guy. He's such a total knock-off.

I continued climbing up the stairs. Aiden rushed to walk next to me. His eyes stared at me, but I refused to stare back.

"Mad?" Aiden asked.

"No," I said bitterly. "I'm very happy I want to fly!"

He wasn't impressed. "Why are you mad? Is it because of me?"

By that time, we were already standing in front of my room. The sight of my room would be a mockery to him. His room might be the size of three rooms joined together.

I opened the door and quickly closed it before Aiden could get it. The door was about to close fully when Aiden pushed his shoe in between. I kicked his shoes and pushed harder. The pain should've been enough for him to pull his shoes out of the way, but he didn't bulge.

"For goodness sake, Aiden, I don't want to see your face right now," I hissed.

Aiden's face appeared on the gap that his shoes created. His eyes showed tiredness. The bandage around his head had turned pinkish now. Despite all these, he was still Aiden: the tall charismatic guy with a beautiful smile. He gave me a sweet smile, his face twisted into a pleading look.

"Let me in, please?" he pleaded.

"Give me one reason why I should let you in," I told him.

"I know you're angry right now. Maybe I can fix you." Aiden widened his billion-dollar smile. I was tempted to quickly open him the door. His smile was persuasive. But then everything came back to me. He lied to everyone. Liars do not receive respect.

"Get out," I said through gritted teeth. I leaned hard on the door and crushed his feet. With all my energy left, I tried to push the door to close. From the other side of the door, I heard Aiden yelped. Before I knew it, his shoe was gone, and my door was fully closed.

I quickly locked myself inside the door. The doorknob moved like someone from outside was trying to force it open. I grinned, satisfied, at my work.

"I can explain," Aiden said. "I know you're pissed, but shouldn't you be happy that your friend over here isn't actually living a poor life?"

"Since when are we even friends?" I said, my words full of venom.

I imagined Aiden cringing on the other side of the wall. A sigh escaped his mouth. "We've always been friends, right? That's why you bother giving me Christmas presents at all," he said. He hesitated for a moment. Inside, I was compensated. I did bother wrapping up Christmas presents for him every year, and just like any other years, he never accepted it. No, he refused to accept it.

"I know I never actually accepted it," he admitted. "But I do appreciate you for that. You're not mad that I never accepted anything that you made. You never give up trying to persuade me receive it."

I gulped. I never gave up. I'm giving up now. He is a lie.

"Listen," he remarked. "I have reasons for that."

I listened.

"Reasons no one will ever understand, that is." He chuckled a bit.

I was bored.

"Does that mean you should lie about your own life? You don't have to lie, Aiden. I want to know why you need to build up this lie, this fake drama about you," I told him.

He was taken aback. "Why do you care?"

Leaning on the door, I slide down the door and sat on the floor. "Because..."

He waited for an answer. I was hoping that he would talk again, speak and try to persuade me to open the door. In reality, I don't have an answer. Why do I even care for this guy? He was nothing to me. Why am I angry that everything about him is a lie? Why am I never satisfied?

"Because," I finally stated. "It's something you don't understand. Knowing it is no use."

"I don't want to be that rich boy at school, Stanza," Aiden said. "I've felt how it felt like to be that rich boy. Life was fake. It was better this way. If I love it this way, why could anyone just love it with me? If people actually care about my feelings, why can't they be happy when I'm happy?"

Do I care for him?

Do I care about his feelings?

"Maybe I don't care for you at all," I concluded.

"That's very unlike you. You care for everyone, even for jerks like me," he said. "Correct?"

Silence.

"Sometimes I think you're too kind. I think of tricking you into one of my infamous plans, but whenever I look back at you, I see something in you that make me halt. Your acceptance for everyone made me respects you. It makes me feel comfortable around you. You don't accept me for my appearance. You see me as me."

I gulped. “I still hate you. You think I care about people, you’re wrong.” But I unlocked the door.

Aiden turned the doorknob and peered his head in. “Hi,” he said, waving with a smile.

“I don’t care about you. You’re wrong,” I told him. I was still seated on the floor. Feeling embarrassed, I hugged my knees as Aiden closed the door and sat beside me.

“It doesn’t matter if you don’t care about me.” He grabbed my face with gentleness. I flushed. The butterflies in my stomach started growling. My eyes focused with his.

“What—“ I was uncomfortable.

“I said, I don’t care if you don’t care me.”

“Then?”

Aiden smiled. “One thing that I know, I do care about you.”

It's a filled chapter :D more soon <3 Love YOU ALL :D

♛ Revealing his identity to the whole world

Yes, I know it's been practically a long time since I even write or update. I'm really sorry for that. My head is about to blow up due to the enormous school projects and the abundance of school tests. Yes, I was almost thinking of burning the school. But to keep in touch with my fellow readers, here's another cahpter for His Rich Highness. I promise to update my other stories soon :(I reach this dead end with Breaking The Cinderella Rules, and trust me, I start to wonder why I even create such characters... Anyway, enjoy the chapter :D dedicated to another of my favorite author on :D

Chapter 5 - Revealing his indentity to the whole world

“One thing that I know, I do care about you.”

As soon as those words left his mouth, I stared at the ground. My heart was hammering like something sharp had just stabbed it, leaving an undeniable pain inside. For a moment, I was immobilized, my head refusing to look up and gaze back at Aiden. I realized he was still sitting beside me.

By now, the gap between us had decreased. I felt him tense beside me as if his senses just came back in. His breathing was getting faster as I mustered enough courage to look into his eyes. He stared back with eyes full of shock.

I cleared my throat. "D—did you just say that?" I asked, incredulous.

He stared at the ceiling. "I'm not sure either."

I narrowed my eyes. "How can you not be sure of the words that come out of your mouth, idiot?"

Aiden grinned. "For your information, I'm not an idiot. I actually passed my IQ test with flying colors."

"Shut up," I snapped.

Then there was silence. Aiden was busy with his own thoughts as he stared at the high ceiling of my room. His tiredness was shown on his face, the bandage around his head making his uncomfortable. Without realizing it, he kept on touching his head, his bandage, like he was confused.

"You okay?" I asked.

He nodded lazily. Slowly, he traced his fingers down his bandage and winced. He paled instantly. "Yes."

I folded my arms. "Convince me."

"I'm fine. I think I'm just too tired. That's why I'm being delirious. Now I'm seeing and saying things I shouldn't have see or told. And I just remembered I have a scheduled appointment with another company on the issue regarding our joined hotel companies. I think I might have dinner with the President of another of our company, and—" He finally slurred. His eyes were getting heavier, and his head almost hit the floor if I wasn't there to catch him.

"Wake up, idiot." I shook his shoulder, but he refused to open his eyes.

"Wake me up in the morning," he mumbled.

"Idiot, dumbass, Mr. Know it all. You think you know it all—"

He smiled. "You sound more like Miss Know It All."

Then he slept.

Giving up, I let his head to rest on my shoulder. My eyes lingered to his face. The features of his face that made him the most gorgeous boy at school emerged into the picture. I was tempted to touch his angular face, his unavoidable lips.

I do care about you.

I laid my head on top of his, and we stayed like that for the rest of the night.

I woke up and felt the comfort of my bed. The memories of last night came filling into my head, and I bolted out of bed, my eyes searching for any trace of Aiden. Questions bombarded my head, and a fresh headache attacked me.

How did I get up here?

Where's Aiden?

Why did he leave without telling?

Why is he such an idiot?

I was about to reach my phone to call him when the screen on my phone showed the time: 7:45 AM.

"HOLY—"

"Well, well, did Miss Rich Girl almost curse?" I flashed the most terrifying glare on whoever said that to me. To my surprise, Aiden was leaning on the door, his face showing pure amusement. He was already dressed neatly like a business man: a white shirt, jeans, and a blue suit. The bandage around his head last night was exchanged with a fresh new one. My eyes didn't felt him until he coughed.

"Don't waste your time to stare at me. You and I have exactly 15 minutes to get ready and go to school," he noted before pointing at me. "And apparently, Miss Rich Girl has not even step one foot into the bathroom."

I glared at him as a wide smile began to crawl up his face. In hilarity, he stuck his tongue out like a little kid. Annoyed, I ran into him, making him stumble and hit himself hard on the ground. He groaned as his head crashed with the floor, but this time, I found little pity to apologize to him.

I grinned with pleasure of his pain. "Yes, yes, make sure you know never to mess with this girl," I said, my face getting closer to his face as I said my threat.

He got rid of the pain easily. Before I knew it, another grin replaced his pained face. "I do whatever I want. After all, I'm Mr. Know It All, correct?" He used his intellectual tone on me, driving me on my nerves.

My hands were about to strangle his precious little neck when he widened his eyes. "We now have 10 minutes to prepare before school starts," he announced. I punched his chest, but it wasn't enough to hurt him. Instead, he laughed as I tried to punch him as hard as I can.

"Do you hate me that much?" he asked, laughing.

I shook my head. "I hate you even more than you think!"

All my punches were useless. "I have lots of practice on pain, my dear Stanza," he mumbled. Then he smirked at me and stared at my position. Just then, heat filled my cheeks. I was sitting on top of him for a long time by now.

"I—I," I started to spell out some words when Aiden lifted himself from the ground, making me tumble to the sides.

Damn, he's strong. He's the school's bad boy after all.

And the heir of almost everything in the entire country.

He didn't look at me as he said, "Get ready. I'll meet your downstairs. I'll be driving your car today, by the way. Your mom insisted that I should come with you to school."

"Who says you can touch my precious car?" I snapped at him.

He grinned. "I say so."

And my patience came to an end.

Aiden drove like a maniac. He was literally driving at 100 km/hour as soon as his hands landed on the steering wheel. The wind blew my hair as the car ran swiftly down the road. From the corner of my eyes, I saw many people giving us the eye for driving above the speed limit. Secretly, I was praying so the police wouldn't figure this out and would leave us alone. I also pray so that Aiden wouldn't end us both in the hospital.

Miraculously, I was still breathing when Aiden parked my car outside of our school. As we both got out of the car, many of the students gave us the stare like we were the newest discovery in the world. Aiden didn't seem to notice the stares people were giving him, or maybe he didn't give a damn about it. He was used to attention. The school had its attention at him after all.

"Stanza!" Rachel screamed my name down the hallway as she ran to me before giving me her favorite deathly hug.

"R—Ra—Rachel—can't—"

She let go off me. "Oh, sorry. I heard you just came to school with Aiden."

Rumors spread that quickly here. "Yeah, I kind of got both of us arrested yesterday—"

Rachel widened her eyes. "This is getting interesting. Spill!"

I shook my head. "Sorry, private information."

She pouted. "So is he going to be your new driver? Is he really that desperate for money?"

If only she knew.

"You would want to be careful of your words toward Aiden, Rachel. He's kind of... scary," I told her.

"How scary?"

"So scary that you could easily be eliminated out of earth with a snap of his fingers," I clarified.

She blinked. "No way, don't tell me he's a killer on the run! This is so getting into the school's newspaper. Our bad boy is a killer on the—"

I sealed Rachel's big mouth with one hand as soon as the people around us started giving us strange looks. "Rachel, keep it down. Let's just get to class," I said.

"But we don't have class today," she said.

I was taken aback. "Why?"

"The school is holding the first orientation program. Apparently, from this year and onwards, the seniors must be friendly around the juniors, and seniors must guide juniors. You name it. So we're going to introduce ourselves one by one to the new students who just transferred today," Rachel explained.

"Students transferred here?" I asked. My school was a prestigious expensive school. Not everyone can enter this school, which was why everyone doubted how Aiden could even step one foot on this school when he looked poor. Everyone had not known his inevitable secret.

Rachel nodded. "Apparently, they're in for scholarship."

"Since when did the school provide scholarships?" I asked.

"Since today," she answered dully.

By then, we have arrived at the conference room. When we both stepped in, huge rows full of comfortable chairs filled our sight. The red and white tall walls appeared in front of us. The school's conference room always mesmerized me. It looked like half a theatre and a half an aula. There was a podium in front of the conference room, and a huge screen was plastered behind the podium like the screen of a theatre.

Most of the seats were already filled. My grade level this year only consisted of 78 students. Rachel and I joined our classmates on the front row of the conference room. Once I was seated on the comfortable leather chair and rested my feet on the footrest, I looked behind me. New students roamed the rows behind. Familiar and new faces emerged. I saw familiar ones, which were probably the children of my father's working partner, but there were new faces.

"Settle down," the principal's assistance, Miss Bone, said through the microphone in the podium. Everyone was quickly seated on their seats as soon as Miss Bone's fierce voice filled the entire area.

"Today the school is holding a new program. From now on, seniors must—" Miss Bone kept on closing and opening her mouth, her words entered my ears, but I failed to recognize anything. I was bored.

"So, let's introduce some of the most important people in the senior level," Miss Bone stated. "Miss Rachel Everlight!"

When Miss Bone said the word Everlight, a wave of whispers was heard from the back side of the conference room. The Everlights was one of the most important families in the whole town. They owned many shops in the shopping center and even helped build our school.

Rachel started introducing herself to the new kids. Before I knew it, some of the other most powerful heirs of important companies were called to introduce themselves. The school just loved to show off their rich students.

"Next, we have Constanza Adeline!"

I froze on my seat.

"Miss Adeline, please stand and introduce yourself to our new students," Miss Bone said. She twitched an evil smile that stated everything out: that's the consequence for judging my event as boring.

I stood up and face the crowd. "My name is Constanza Adeline." My mind raced as I tried to think of any other words to say. "I'm the heir to one of the most famous hotels in the country, and I'll be glad to help my peers in any way. And by the way, I love to give out gifts during Christmas. I gave my presents away yesterday."

I cleared my throat. "So, I hope you all have a nice time in your new school!" I quickly sat down. Many of my classmates were giving me thumbs up, showing that they were proud of me. My stress was almost off my shoulders when something bigger came to the picture frame.

"The Principal apologized for not being here today. Due to many businesses and problems, a representative would be saying the Principal's message for the new students. Please clap for the heir of the Skyler Group!" Miss Bones said.

This was the defining moment.

Everyone would know who Aiden was.

This would be the end of his rumor of being sickly poor.

Whispers flooded the entire room. They surely never heard that the heir of the Skyler Group was enrolled in our school. It's all because everyone looked down on his as the poor kid. Everyone treated him like trash.

"Mr. Skyler, please stand. Your grandfather insisted," Miss Bone said.

A wave of gasps filled my ears as a figure stood up from his head. Rachel who was sitting behind me was ready to pull her eyes off their sockets. "H—how can this be true?" she asked.

"My name is Aiden Skyler," Aiden started regardless of the murmurs around him. "I'm the heir of the Skyler Group, which is where

I'm working at now. If my grandfather is here today, he would've given you all a long speech on how to success in this school. The key of success lies in two points: study hard and join the crowd. Well, unless you have a specific reason to hide your identity."

Everyone stared with disbelief as Aiden sat back down on his seat. The people around him gave him the eyes that clearly screamed You're a liar!

"Thank you, Aiden, for your words. Aiden is one of the most successful people who had studied in our board of studies. He's now the CEO of the Skyler Group—"

The whole room was heating.

"The Skyler Group owned basically almost all the markets in our country. They owned the gas stations, the malls, the—"

The room was a microwave.

"And Aiden Skyler is now officially the heir of the Skyler's Group's entire assets."

And then a roar of protests filled the conference room.

Thank you everyone for reading. Just in case you found typos, please tell me. I have not proofread or fixed mistakes on this... I don't have time to do it... I have to create a report! >< ahh !!! school just officially sucks.

♛ The truth that cursed his life

Hello, readers of His Rich Highness! Here's an early update on Aiden and Stanza's journey. I'm trying to focus on Aiden's past right now. Well, although he's super rich, he has one hard life. It's all like Breaking the Cinderella Rules. I'm trying to focus on the past of the main male protagonist of all my stories. <3 Now here's a chapter on Aiden's life! I hope you like it

Again, dedicated to the awesome author in :D

All around the world

People want to be loved

They're not different than us

-All Around the World by Justin Bieber

Chapter 6 –The truth that cursed his life

"That's bullshit," one of the students called.

I cringed as Aiden was taunted by a wave of protests. Even Rachel looked at his direction with enough fierce intensity to kill a monster. The whole room erupted, disbelieving the whole truth. A few boys got up from their seats and started for Aiden. My heart leaped as one of the boys rushed his way to Aiden before landing one fist on his cheek.

Aiden didn't even shrink. He quickly deflected the punch away from his face. A gasp escaped my mouth as I saw Aiden's true nature. He was a math genius. Calculating his opponent's attack and all the angles, he was able to keep up with the violence all around him. More students started to lunge at him. Exasperated, I saw him took a step and stood on his own seat.

"Stop!" he screamed, his eyes showing deep fury.

Some of the students cowered as his terrifying glance landed on them. From the stage, Miss Bones looked pleased as everyone quieted down. Rachel tensed as I kept my eyes on Aiden from my seat.

"Why are you all protesting?" he asked. "I know this all sounds so surreal, but this is who I am. Those gossips you made about me are fake. This is the real me. Now accept that fact, or you and I will have a problem."

Whispers echoed in the huge aula. Beside me, Rachel was unimpressed. "I have a question," she called in the middle of the whispers. Everyone stopped their small chitchat and focused their attention on her. Rachel gripped her seat tightly, and I held my breath for what's going to come next.

"I don't care that you're the freaking heir of the enormous Skyler Group Company, but I have a question that's bugging me. If you're that rich, why hide the fact that you're one wealthy guy? Why the big secret?"

Most of the students nodded their heads, agreeing with her question. Aiden shook his head, the intensity of his eyes decreasing. “Even if I tell you the answer, you wouldn’t be able understand it. It’s too complicated. Life is intricate after all,” he confessed.

“Fine, then it’s not problem if you tell us. After all, we won’t understand. Explain it to us, maybe we will understand,” Rachel pressed on.

“Sometimes things are better to stay secret,” Aiden said. “Sometimes telling the secret means reopening the scar someone had tried so badly to close.”

Rachel snorted and folded her arms. “What scar do you have? You’re filthy rich. Your parents must have pampered you since you’re born. What can possibly go wrong in your family?”

Aiden bowed his head. I could see he was debating to either tell everyone the truth or not. The answer was coming. I knew it. Last night, when I asked him the same question, he didn’t fully answer me.

“It’s not that easy,” he whispered.

“Nonsense,” Rachel retorted. “You’re a whole lie, a total piece of—“

“Rachel,” I interrupted. “Please stop.”

She blinked at me. “Stanza, are you helping that liar?”

“He must have his own reasons,” I told her silently.

Rachel furrowed her forehead and masked her enraged expression. “I don’t get it, Constanza.” I grimaced as she called my full name.

"What?" I asked. "Not everyone have a perfect life. Even in a family that has everything they need, there must at least be a defect inside, a small crack that you can't see unless you go inside."

Rachel huffed. "I can't believe you prefer him than your own best friend," she spat. Before I could say another word, she got up from her and stormed out. By now, every pair of eyes was staring back at me. I would've thrown up due to all the stares and my nervousness if Aiden didn't took a shortcut by walking on the seats to reach me.

I looked up at him. "What—"

I stopped my words when he gave me a hand. He gently pulled my hand into his, and for the first time, I felt genuine warmth from him. Slowly, I was pulled of my seat until I was actually standing on my own seat, my hand enclosed with his.

Everyone gasped, and the ladies looked in turn to glare at me. Aiden was in fact a school star despite his reputation as poor. Now the tables were flipped. He was a bigger star than before, but his reputation was rearranged. He wasn't the poor kid. He was a liar, a very handsome liar.

"Let's go out," he whispered in my ear. He gestured his head to the exit. "Lead the way, my lady."

I blushed as he called me my lady. He was trying to charm me. If any other boys try to charm me for something they wanted, I would've kicked them hard on the face, but Aiden was an exception. He had this aura around his that told me to stay calm and follow his orders. Somehow by being near him, I was sure that he was going to lead me in the right direction. Holding his hand, I walked my way through the soft red cushions to the exit.

Miss Bones and the rest of the remaining students didn't say a word as Aiden and I pushed the double doors, exiting the aula. Once we were out, we let go out our desperate breath. We were gasping hard when the cold wind embraced us.

Outside the windows of our school, snow had piled up in the roads. Crystals of something white and soft were floating in the air, falling from the grey sky to the ground before they melt and join the sea of white snow. I shivered in the cold as Aiden pulled my hand. Without protesting, I followed his guide.

"Where are we going?" I asked him.

"We're going to a very tall tower to eat, Stanza," he proposed.

I frowned. "Why am I coming?"

He grinned. "Because you're my only friend and I need someone to talk to? Duh." He face-palmed me.

My cheeks flushed as his hand brushed my cheek. His grip tightened on me as we reached the outside world, the road full of thick snow. He smiled at me before helping me walk across the snow. Our shoes created freshly made prints on the ground, the blankets of snow. My teeth chattered as the coldness started to seep into my skin, making my hands quiver slightly.

When I noticed we were heading out of school and into a public bus stop, I asked him, "Don't you have a car?"

He shook his head. "I don't like cars. They give me nightmares."

I smirked. "So Mr. Know It All is finally vulnerable to something."

His eyes darkened, and I knew I just said something wrong. "I'm sorry," I quickly apologized. Aiden looked into my eyes, his blue eyes reflecting sadness towards me. Then he smiled softly.

"I'm fine," he said. We were now standing in front of the bus stop, staring at the empty land across the road. More snow fell from the sky, drenching both of us. I trembled. The coldness was too much to bear. Aiden, after noticing me, took of his own suit and handed it to me.

"Wear it," he said, something like smoke appeared as he spoke.

"You're cold." I scrutinized his face to look for any affects of the coldness on him.

Aiden shrugged. "I'm used to being cold."

"Why?"

He smiled weakly. "My parents were strict, you know. Even though we live in a sufficient family, I was trained to be obedient. One wrong word and I might suffer a day outside the gates. No matter how extreme the condition outside can be, they would throw me out of the house. I learn to embrace any situation, although I got sick after that."

He chuckled, but I grimaced. "Do you hate them for that?" I asked him.

"I did, at first. It was when they're gone out of my life that I learn to understand why they punished me harshly," he admitted.

I gasped. "Your parents—they're not here anymore?"

He shook his head. "They died in a car accident. When they died, all the assets would be surrendered to either my hands or any other of the family members. I was only eligible to take all the assets when I'm 16. That's why my other family members tried desperately to steal everything I had. No one cared for me.

"I was almost taken to a foster home when my dad's younger brother almost took everything. They tried to steal the whole company, ignoring the fact that I would be losing everything. Through that moment of my life, I realized no one truly cared for me, that all the affection given by other people were just charms to get whatever they wanted," he continued.

Aiden sighed. "My 16th birthday eventually came, and I was eligible to retrieve everything back. Of course, my uncle tried thousands of ways to prevent me to take it back. He tried to make me suffer. Sometimes I see strange people coming at me, trying to beat the crap out of me, but everything my parents taught me came back reeling in my head. I learn to fight back through all the pain and suffering I had at home. Then I realized all the tears I've cried when my parents are still there was to protect me. They were trying to build me so I would be as hard as diamond. So that when something goes wrong, I can reclaim my place back."

"And you did," I completed for him.

He bobbed his head. "It was hard. Everything was so complicated, but I managed to hack the whole company's system from inside. I know it sounded impossible, but I'm really good at hacking. I might sound stupid at school, but in reality, I wasn't just up to it at school. I got into this troublesome court for destroying all the efforts my uncle made. I wanted revenge. My uncle hired more expensive lawyers to defend his opposition, while I was left with no one, rotting in a dirty cell for a month. If my parents' old lawyer didn't come to offer me a hand, I would've spent my whole life in jail. Yeah, I was too stubborn. I needed revenge. Mr. Clark, the lawyer, was one of the expert lawyers in the whole world. I was able to retrieve all the Skyler Group assets back into my hands, and now, Mr. Clark's my caretaker."

I widened my eyes in disbelief. I did heard that Aiden was missing from school for a few months, but I never imagined that he was actually in the state of life or death, begging behind the bars. The image of little Aiden being handcuffed inside a holding cell made me shiver. Anything could happen inside: fights and abuse. It was a miracle that he was still sane.

"I'm sorry," I tried to make him calm.

He shook his head. "Through that experience, I learn to depend on my own instincts. I have to choose the right people to trust. I can't trust anyone that easily anymore. Deep trust can crush you to the bones."

"So you own the whole company now?" I asked.

He nodded.

"Who's taking care of our school?"

"Definitely not a family members. I have a few people appointed to take care of each department of the Skyler Group assets. They're not family, but I learn to trust them for they defended me together with Mr. Clark in court. I was in the most desperate situation, but they were there for me. They were my parents' friends, and my parents' friends are like legal guardians to me," he said simply.

The bus came to a halt when they driver saw us standing on the bus stop. Aiden entwined our hands again as he got into the bus. I sat beside him. Slowly, the bus took off.

“We’re going into the city,” I noticed.

He nodded. “I’m taking you to a journey of my life.”

“Why?”

“We’re still having that anthropology project, are we? You can learn about love from my life,” he said.

Of course we could learn love from his life. We could learn of love, harsh love, from him. His parents’ love and cautiousness shaped him. Now he was incapable of loving intently due to all his experiences. “Let’s see if I can love someone deeply,” he said.

“Who?” I asked curiously.

“Let’s see if I can care for you deeply, Stanza. Let’s give love a try.”

Thank you people for reading! I would probably update again on December :(I'm going to have my finals soon, and projects are starting to pile up. I'll try my best to update as fast as possible :D

My replay of Titanic

Hello, my beloved readers! Thank you for always reading His Rich Highness. I'm finally done with my exams. Here's another update on Aiden and Stanza :) I hope you guys like it :D We're going to reach the end soon in about 5 chapters, more or less. Please don't give up on this story! I will update as soon as possible since I'm now having my holiday!

Chapter 7—My replay of Titanic

Snow poured from the sky, frosting the window of the bus. My fingers traced the appearing shape of a snowflake on the clear view of the window. Its intricate pattern surprised me, forming a smile on my lips. As I jotted the structure of the snowflake, I felt the cold transfer from the outside to my skin. Coldness seeped into my skin, giving me tingles. I squeezed my hands together in an effort to warm myself.

Beside me, Aiden was looking forward towards the window at the other side. He was thinking to himself, perhaps about his life and how sadistic it had been. My heart still ached when I reminisced his story in my mind. The way he changed his tone when he told it to me, how it turned from a sigh to an emotionless tone, I remembered every single detail, and the remembrance brought more sadness into me.

Suddenly, his body shook, and he sighed.

I placed a hand on his shoulder. "You okay?" I asked.

He hesitated before nodding slowly. "Never felt better."

Before we could say anything else, the bus came to a halt. Aiden quickly searched for my hand and stood up. I glanced at the windows. Tall buildings covered the entire block. Expensive shops with branded stocks appeared into view. "Get up, we're here," Aiden said, gesturing me to stand up.

I got up and followed him out of the bus. "Where are we going?"

The sun was slowly shutting down, giving the sky a reddish tint to it. My eyes scanned around the road. People bustled around us, squeezing us. Some of them glared at us for stopping in the middle of the street. Cars passed by beside us.

"We're going to have dinner," he concluded. A smirk formed on his face, and he gently squeezed my hand. "Any ideas for our project?"

I rolled my eyes. "The last time I had an idea you decided to ignore it, and we ended up in the police station. Are you sure you want to here it?"

He grinned. "That was only partially my fault. It's not my mistake that you're kind of impatient."

I playfully punched his shoulder, irritated. "You arrogant guy," I spat.

"But you like me."

My stubbornness relented, and I blushed slightly. "Who says I like you?" I demanded.

He laughed. "Please, it's written all over your face."

"Really? Last time I checked, I don't write a thing on my face." I clicked my tongue, completely pleased with my response.

"I remember you were constantly looking at me at class. Your sleepy eyes would snap open once I bang the door and walk inside the classroom. You would blush when I irritate you. I can't believe how easy I change your emotions, and then it becomes a game to me to make you angry. You're too cute when you're angry," he admitted. His speech made my flush, the red tint in my cheeks becoming obvious that his eyes widened.

"See? It's that easy!" He admired his own ability, and I punched him again. "Now, now, don't be violent," he said, smiling.

I have no idea how many times I rolled my eyes at him today. It would probably take forever to count, but the fact amused me. I couldn't imagine not having him with me today, or any other days I was with him. He made my day colorful, and I made his day cheerful. Together, we gave a slight smile on each other's broken hearts.

A few days ago, I would be a normal girl sitting around school, staring Aiden like some kind of lonely monster, but since the love project, my love line turned a 360 turn. I've dug deeper into Aiden more than he thought I did. I realized that we shouldn't judge people from the appearance, for their hearts create a huge difference.

The sky turned completely dark. I stumbled as we walked toward a tall building. Aiden quickly caught me before shaking his head. "Careless," he muttered, "very careless."

I pulled myself away from him and pouted. "Accident happens everywhere."

He laughed but continued to guide me into the tallest tower in the city. My heart accelerated as we squeezed through the bustling crowd. Aiden pushed me closer to him. I accidentally brushed his skin and flinched. He gave me a questioning look but continued to push into the crowd.

"We're here," he said, releasing my hand. Secretly, I was disappointed that he let to go of my hand. The comfortable sensation he gave me when he held my hand was undeniably enjoyable.

"Welcome to the SKYLER's group best restaurant, located at the top of the highest tower in town," he stated proudly. By then, we stood below the roof of a rocketing tower. Its top seemed to be hidden by the clouds that were scattered in the sky.

Aiden told something one of the waiters in front of the entrance, and then, the waiter motioned us to step into an elevator. One side of the elevator was made of glass, showing the view outside the elevator. I stepped together with Aiden into the lift, careful not to trip again. The waiter pressed the button to go to the highest floor, the 105th floor.

Fear crept into me as the elevator began to move straight up. I saw the people below turned smaller and smaller as the elevator rocketed like a mini plane to the sky. I shivered at the view of the city that began to turn into small dots of lights. Aiden chuckled when he found me clutching the railings around the elevator for support. When I looked down from the elevator, my head began to spin crazily.

Aiden placed both hands on my shoulder. I could tell that his face was just an inch away from me as he leaned into me. "Everything's going to be alright," he whispered. I could feel his breath, his warmth. Then everything seemed comfortable, nice and warm. I sighed in relief as the elevator began to decelerate before stopping at the correct floor, 105 floors above the ground.

The doors of the elevator opened, showing an elegant dinner room. There were other people eating at the place. The dim lighting and glassed surrounding gave a romantic feeling to it. Everything looked too elegant. The tables were covered with white, and a rose was place in the middle.

A waitress quickly caught up with us and guided us to a place for two in one edge of the restaurant. We ordered some food with skyrocketing prices, and then, I grabbed my laptop to start working on our essay project. Ideas emerged, and Aiden typed it on my laptop. His sentences surprised me. Every single sentence was full of new vocabularies for me. He described love as a catalyst. It changed people, but love itself remained unchanged.

The whole essay was done in less than an hour, and when I scanned through it, checking for grammar or spelling mistakes, I found none. Aiden was incredibly talented in writing. In front of me, he was munching on a red velvet macaroon, looking through the glass that showed us a beautiful view of the world around us.

"Okay, this is a good essay, but I think we're missing a huge conclusion," I said.

Aiden wrinkled his forehead. "That is?"

"The conclusion of what love is. It can be many things: warmth, a companion, a catalyst, healing—"

"Love can be many things. That's why love isn't just affection or kindness, or anything in this world. Love is beyond the material things we see. Love is invisible, yet we feel it. It is indescribable and indestructible. Love is the key to an entrance to a completely different world, a world where anything is possible," he said.

I smiled. "Love is the moment when we hold our hands together, when we brush into each other, when we stared into each other's eyes. It is the moment when we eat, breathe, and live together."

"Exactly! That's why love is a whole new world," he concluded. "When we're in love, it's like we're in a whole different world. That's why not everyone understands. Only those who had embrace the world of love can fully acknowledge how important it is to love and be kind."

He typed in more words into my laptop before suddenly closing it.

"Love feels nice," he said in all of a sudden.

He stared into me, catching my attention. I smiled and blushed. "It does," I replied. "Love is nice."

The moment became warmer and warmer. Before I knew it, our faces came closer. He was inches away from me, closing in the distance upon us. I could feel his breath, and my heart was pounding. I closed my eyes, waiting for the impact of his lips crashing into mines.

It was getting closer, too close to be true. His lips brushed into mines, and my heart jumped in surprise. It was just a slight brush, but it made my heart bloom. And I knew I wanted more, fiercer and more intense—

"Excuse me?"

We quickly parted. A waitress stood in front of us, staring at us awkwardly. "Here's the bill," she said, emotionless. Aiden's cheeks were as red as mines as he took a credit card from his wallet before handing it towards her.

"Should I pay too?" I asked, my hand searching for the wallet inside my disorganized bag.

Aiden shook his head. "All on me," he said, smiling.

It took the waitress exactly 45 seconds to come back and ushered us out of the restaurant. Some of the waiters quickly acknowledged Aiden as we walk back into the elevator. He was the owner of the restaurant after all. Some of the waitress blushed as his gaze landed on them. Aiden smiled weakly at them, and I frowned.

We got into the elevator, and the waitress pressed the button to the ground floor. The doors closed, and the elevator began to descend down.

"Thanks for tonight," I told him as the view outside began to enlarge.

He smiled. "You're welcome."

Then there was silence.

I stared at the beautiful view outside. Aiden held one of my hands, and suddenly, the fear of heights was gone out of my list of fears. I wasn't afraid when he was with me. The mesmerizing view outside trapped me in wonders.

"It's all so beautiful," I mumbled to myself.

Aiden then wrapped his arms around my waist. I almost jumped from his action if he didn't calm me down, soothing me. With his arms around me, the elevator descended. The act reminded me of Titanic. Rose was spreading her arms, and Jack was holding on to her. Now, I was dumbfounded, a smile growing too evidently on my face. Aiden was holding on to me, circling his arms around me. The view of the outside world made the whole event even more romantic.

I blushed when he suddenly turned me around so that I was facing him. Then our lips crashed. This time there was no one to interrupt us. I felt his soft lips on mines, biting each single breath. And then I knew I wanted even more. The kiss turned harsher, and we were both breathless by the time the elevator reached the ground floor.

We parted once the doors opened, and he held out a hand to me.

"Let's go?" he asked, a genuine smile forming on his lips.

I took his hand, and we walked out the elevator, holding hands like nothing in this world can break us apart.

Yeah, I'm really bad at kiss scenes... see you guys again, soon! :D And remember Stanza's words... "Accidents happen everywhere." :p Yes, this is a clue, my friend! I just realized I never actually gave Stanza's and Aiden's school a name...

You drive me crazy

Hello, there :) Here's an early update on His Rich Highness. I got stuck in writing Breaking the Cinderella rules, so I decided to finish this story quickly so I can fully focus on my other story :) This is a filler chapter... I'm sorry if it sucks a lot :(

Chapter 8—You drive me crazy

My hand never left his, which was weird. I've never lingered around someone for this long, and I think I've never got this much affection from anyone I know. This comfort that surrounds me was new. It seemed to tell me it was okay to step out of my own comfort zone. I felt his warmth crawling into my skin when he looked at me and smiled. And I couldn't help but smile back.

How could I be this girl? How does he easily influence me?

I was too infatuated with him that I was going crazy.

Yeah, that's why.

As soon as we got out of the SKYLER group's best restaurant, a red Ferrari appeared into view and stopped in front of us. Aiden gestured me to go in. I hesitated when he opened the door for me.

"C'mon, let's go," he ushered me into the car. He gave me a hand, and I took it.

"I thought you hate cars," I pointed out and then felt guilty the next second after those words were out of my mouth.

Aiden smiled weakly. "It's fine." I let go of his hand as soon as I was seated inside the car. Aiden sighed as he placed his fingers on the steering wheel, probably unsure if he should do this or not. "We all have to face our fears, right?" he finally asked.

I darkened. "It's okay to have fears. No one's perfect."

He turned on the engine, and before I could take a deep breath, the car lurched. The street disappeared into view in a blink of an eye. When I turned back, I saw the lights of the city started to dim as Aiden drove farther out of the city. Snow was pouring heavily from the sky that was too dark to be true.

"Where are we going now?" I glanced out of the window. When I looked over at him, I saw his fingers trembled on the steering wheel. His eyes were focused on the road like something could go wrong if he pushed his gaze away for just a second.

"Hey," I called. "Relax, nothing's going to go wrong."

"That's what my Dad used to say. Nothing will ever go wrong. But everything went wrong on the very night he said that," he confessed.

I stared at him for a moment. "I'm afraid, Stanza," he said.

"Goodness, you're being too dramatic." I grinned. "And here I thought I was the good girl full of fear."

He rolled his eyes.

"Where are we going anyway?" I asked.

"A place full of lights," he easily answered.

I checked my clock. "It's 10 PM right now. Shouldn't we just go home?"

He looked at me like I was crazy, but then quickly averted his gaze back to the road. "What's wrong with 10 PM?"

"I should be home before 9!"

Aiden shook his head. "Haven't you learn anything from me? I never go home before midnight. Why bother to anyway?"

I punched him playfully. "For your information, I'm a good girl, not like you, Mr. Know It All."

He brushed his own shoulder. "I think I'm going to bruise. Do you know how many times you've punched me? It's hurting you know."

Rolling my eyes, I punched him again, harder this time and probably too harsh. Suddenly, Aiden's hands left the steering wheel, and the car lurched to the other side of the road, into the middle of nowhere. He quickly grabbed back the steering wheel, but the car was lurching too sharply, starting to tilt. I gripped Aiden's shoulder, and I pulled him away from the wheel.

"Stanza!" he screamed.

No, no, are we going through an accident?

Nothing is going to go wrong. Now my own words mocked me in the face.

Somehow, Aiden managed to get his hands back, and then, the car was back on the road, safe and smooth.

From the corner of his eyes, he glared at me. "Never ever do that again," he said.

I shrunk deeper into my seat, and he shook his head. "Sorry," I apologized.

"You're so weird, Stanza. You drive me crazy, sometimes. How can I ever understand you?"

"You'll have to try," I said softly.

"I am trying, and I think I'm making a good progress. My conclusion is just you're too crazy to be true. You're too childish, Stanza."

I pouted. "I'm not childish!"

"Let me ask you some questions. Do you believe in Santa?" he asked.

"I—I don't."

"You hesitated," he indicated.

"No, I didn't!" I protested.

"Do you believe in happy endings?"

"Well, I'll have to say yes to that."

He shook his head. "Life is harsh, girl. Be ready for that. Do you believe in Mickey Mouse?"

I narrowed my eyes. "Mickey is my life."

"And here I concluded you're Minnie Mouse, definitely too childish for her own good," he muttered.

"Unless you want this car to tilt again, I need you to stop commenting on me, Aiden." I gritted my teeth.

He laughed. "You're too naïve."

I was about to kill him, but then the car stopped. "We're here," he informed. Then he got out of the car. As soon as the cold wind from the outside world hit my skin, I shivered and crossed my arms. Aiden was already walking ahead of me. Sheltered from the moon's light by the tall pine trees, I looked around in case something might lurk in the darkness. When I heard something howled, I quickly ran, only to hit into Aiden.

He grinned. "Scared?"

"Jerk," I murmured. He grabbed my hand and squeezed it.

We walked like that, into the darkness. He held my hand, again, and whenever I flinched, he would pull me closer into him. I didn't know how long we've been walking pointlessly, but before I could protest, a bridge came into view.

"Ready?" Aiden asked.

I gulped.

He took a step into the bridge, and as soon as he did, lights flickered on the railings of the bridge. I gasped as the environment turned colorful. Lights with different colors like the lighting in a Christmas tree appeared everywhere. The pine trees were decorated like a real Christmas tree, and streetlights appeared into view, lighting our way.

"Look down," he commanded, and I instantly looked the way he told me. A view of the whole city appeared. I stared, my mouth opened in amazement.

"It's so beautiful." I didn't hesitate at all. Aiden was one of the most romantic guys I've ever met.

"I know," he said. "My mom used to take me here."

"My parents rarely talk to me, actually," I admitted. "My mom talks, a lot, but we've never talked about things deep. Do you get it?"

"Yeah," he said.

"My parents are funny, but sometimes I wondered if they have to choose work or their own daughter, would they choose me?"

"That's the pain of being a part of a rich family. Everyone was always away," Aiden said. "People sees us like the luckiest person in the world, but in reality, the richer we became, the colder we became. There was more competition, and the cruelty of the world became too visible. We just gave to bare with it, I guess."

"I'm weak, Aiden. That's fact."

"That's why you have a friend, to strengthen you," he confirmed.

"Who's my friend?" I asked. "I think Rachel hates me now."

He glowered. "I'm sorry."

I instantly shook my head. "No, it's not your fault."

"I know who can be your friend now," he said.

"Who?"

He smiled. "You're looking at him now."

I looked at him in the eye. "Really?"

He nodded.

"Then we need friendship bracelets!"

He pushed me away. "Never mind, we're not friends."

I glared at him. "Mean."

"I am. But you still like me, correct?"

"I hate you sometimes," I blurted. "But you're so hard to ignore."

"That's why I'm unique."

And I punched him again, this time with a smile on my face.

He made me crazy.

I made him crazy.

We drove each other crazy.

And it was fun.

I cherished the moment as Aiden brought my hand closer to him and kissed it.

"Let's be best friends, Stanza," he said. "Best friends forever."

I blushed. "BFFFL?"

He gave me a questioning look.

"Best friends forever for life!"

"Nah, best friends forever for eternity."

And then he pulled me into the warmest hug in my entire life.

I never knew that the tables would turn around, very soon, but for the moment, I cherished the moment with him.

In his arms, I felt safe and secure.

Too madly in love.

Little Talks with myself

Another filler chapter :) But this time, we have AIDEN'S POV!! :D More sarcasm and funny things here. I hope this chapter doesn't ruin the mood for the next chapter. This is going to be a happy goofy chapter, but the next chapter will drop you emotional ;) come and read! I will be updating really soon :) Clue for next chapter: "Accidents happen anywhere." Stanza did say that in the last chapter, right? or did she?

Chapter 9—Little Talks with myself

Aiden's POV

She was beside me, her head facing the window. Although she complained how tired she was due to our little adventure all day, her face told me the opposite: she was actually having fun. Sure, some of the colors had drained from her face as she slept inside the car, but a smile hung on her face, refusing to be torn down.

My hands trembled as I placed my fingers on the steering wheel, but I started getting used to the usual feeling I felt when I drove around the city. With just a little bit of hesitation, I started the engine and drove away from the bridge. Tall pine tress bordered the road in the forest, covering some of the light from the moon.

Soon, the city came into view. All the buildings seemed to be playing their competition, a contest to see who can pass through the clouds. The Ferrari sped up, and I gave us a turn around the city. Lights shone the way, and I followed slowly behind.

A few days ago, I wouldn't be too delighted when our teacher picked Stanza to be my partner on this stupid project. Associating with people wasn't just my thing, and I would prefer to be alone. My trust for people disappeared completely, and I became too paranoid on the fact that everyone was cold and heartless. That's why I was surprised how she easily made me relent, how she easily changed our moods.

Our little talks started to grow, and eventually, we didn't think about the project anymore. She was trying to fix me, to mend me to be able to trust again. I'm not sure how she did it, but she was the first person I started trusting again. Somehow, she persuaded me to tell her my little dirty secrets, unraveling who I really was and tending me from the misery I've been through.

The thought of my past made me quiver, and I made the Ferrari accelerate even more. Cold wind brushed against my skin as opened the window. Despite the icy winter season, I pushed a hand out. The coldness fueled me with energy. Gusts of wind brushed against my skin. I smiled. This was the feeling of freedom: to be free to do anything you want, anything dangerous and anything beautiful.

Stanza bandaged the fragments of my heart. She kept me whole again, and now I felt safer than before.

Lights from the city soon dimmed, and a neighborhood emerged out of nowhere. Huge mansions covered the entire land. Little parks and gardens separated each house from another, making the neighborhood a perfect peaceful place. This neighborhood clearly spelled out "rich" by the looks of the houses and the expensive cars parked outside.

Unconsciously, I turned the radio on and was quickly amused when TalkMusic came blasting from the speakers. To fix the mood, the radio decided to give us a romantic song. Stanza was still asleep, uncaring of anything else in the world and all the trouble it gave her.

I stirred the car to the left, to the direction of Stanza's mansion. A huge gate greeted us. Suddenly, she stirred awake. "We're home?" she asked.

"You're home. I'm not," I informed.

"That's not fair," she said.

I rolled my eyes. "Of course it's not. You're right here, a few steps away from bed, while I still have 15 minutes of driving to TalkMusic."

"You're not going home?" she questioned.

"Got business to do. Now shoo, go out," I commanded, "before I drag you myself."

She pouted. "I don't want to go home."

Her words shocked me. "Why?"

"It's not welcoming anymore. C—can I stay somewhere else for tonight?" she pleaded.

I hesitated. "Well, I'm not going home. Unless you want to come with me to TalkMusic, I won't mind."

She smiled and then drifted back to sleep. I blinked, unknowing her answer. Maybe it was a yes. I pulled away from her house and started racing against the surface of the hard ground. Although Stanza was currently the sweetest thing in my life, she could be quite annoying.

Before she knew it, I parked my car in front of the radio station. Slowly, I nudged her. She looked at me with sleepy eyes before blinking a few times. Then Stanza registered everything. She sat straight on her seat and unbuckled her seatbelt.

"Radio station!" she giggled playfully.

I shook my head as I got out of the car. By then, Stanza was already sprinting towards the building. I locked the car and followed behind her with a soft smile on my face. Her hair was disheveled from our journey, but whenever she looked at me, I couldn't help but admire how beautiful she was.

Those eyes refused to look away from me. Her cheeks grew a faint red tint, and her lip was too pink to be true. When she smiled, cute dimples appeared on the side of her mouth.

"Why are you smiling at me like that?" she suddenly brought up. A blush colored her cheeks.

"Your look like a monster," I pointed out.

She blinked, confused.

"Your hair, my lady," I told her and pushed her into the building where mirrors were available. It took her one second to look into a mirror before her hands started fixing her hair. She collected her hair into one grip before making it flow to one side of her shoulder.

I asked for her hand and entangled my fingers with hers. She gaped at me, and I just smirked with my usual signature smirk. "Let's go." I quickened our pace into the elevator. Pressing the button to go to the 15th floor, I pulled her closer into me. The doors closed, and silence drifted between us.

The elevator sounded a bell tone, indicating that we were here. Soon, the doors opened, showing a long all way. I gestured at her to go out. After all, ladies always come first. The elevator doors almost cut me into half if I didn't quickly exited the lift.

"This is perhaps your office?" Stanza's voice chimed into my ears.

I pointed to the edge of the hallway the only glassed door was attached to the creamy walls. A sign with silver color was placed beside the door. Stanza traced her fingers on the sculptured name on the sign, my name.

"Whoa," she muttered as her eyes scanned my job description right below my name. "CEO of the SKYLER group," she beamed as she said it. "That's cool. If you're the CEO, who's the owner?"

I was surprised by how attentive she was. "Someone I know and someone I can easily bring down if he decided to do anything stupid. He's just a puppet."

She punched my shoulder, and I laughed. "That's not funny!" she retorted. "You just called someone a puppet."

"Fine, let me rephrase that. He's someone I use," I rephrased.

She narrowed her eyes. "That sounds even worst. In fact, it sounds—"she shivered—"so wrong."

I patted her on the back and pulled the glass door open. "Welcome to my second home," I welcomed her. Once she stepped inside my office, a gasp escaped her lips.

"This is crazy!" she screamed. She jumped and landed herself on the soft couches inside my office. Her hands grabbed the little poor plushie I had kept, strangling it as she examined how cute it was.

I laughed. "This is why I told you're childish."

"This is normal!" she argued.

I ignored her. "I'm going to have a meeting," I announced. "You'll stay here and watch out for trouble."

"You have a meeting? This is midnight!" she informed.

"It is, after all, an international business matter." I pulled the door but turned myself back for a moment. "Don't do anything stupid," I warned. I bobbed my head towards the TV. "Go watch something," I suggested.

She gave me a thumbs-up, and I sighed in relief. I could trust her now.

Can I?

I laughed at my own doubt and quickly regretted it when my stomach began to ache from too much laughing. Stepping inside the elevator, I pushed the down button and let the elevator take me to the floor I've chosen. When the door opened, I let go of a sigh and twisted my personality back to the cold serious Aiden Skyler. It was business after all. Funny jokes don't work in this world.

Some of the employee gave me smiles, and I returned them back. Business partners were already seated in the meeting room, together with high-positioned employees. The double door that was the only way out of the meeting room automatically closed as soon as I entered the meeting room. Every single person instantly stood up. I bowed slightly before greeting and telling them to sit back down.

"Thank you for coming," I greeted formally. My hands quickly reached for the files that were stacked in front of me. "Our first problem is—"

My mouth started talking about different things, and protests echoed here and there. We settled agreements, and our ideas were mixed together, forming the most ideal plan.

"This is for the growth of the SKYLER group itself," one of the stockholder demanded.

I nodded, taking his opinion into consideration.

Then waves full of problems filled the rest of my night.

Now the only thing I wanted was to crawl back into my office and sleep.

Remember my warning, guys... "Accident happens everywhere..." Astrid out ;) for now..

♛ Our love that is bleeding

Hello, people! I'm finally home from a trip to Singapore :D Here's another chapter of His Rich Highness. We're reaching the end very very very soon, my friends! :D Just one more chapter (or two if I can make two) to go and the tale of our Stanza and Aiden will come to an end :) Please bare with me. I will update as soon as possible. Four votes or more and I'll update quickly, deal? :p Thank you for all the support guys :D Thank you so much <3

-Astrid

Chapter 10—Our love that is bleeding

He was taking forever, and by the time he entered his office, I was replaying the destruction of titanic in his very own office. The silence surrounding me was making me crazy, and I decided to watch the TV. My hand was about to reach the small remote control when my arm suggested on bumping into a flower vase, making it crash into pieces as soon as it landed on the ground.

Then I realized it wouldn't be a good idea to watch TV. My eyes landed on a small plushie toy, and I accidentally throw it too hard, not knowing I was aiming for the TV screen. And yeah, the whole screen fell. Now, I was wondering how Aiden's face would look like if he saw this whole mess, and that was exactly when the door creaked open, showing Aiden's horrified face.

"What the—" He couldn't even finish his sentence, or his curse. His eyes scrutinized the damages done on his office, and a frown crawled up his face. Shivers ran down my skin, and I gulped as I waited for a scolding or anything of the sort. I was paralyzed when he opened his mouth to say something but closed it again when he saw his TV screen lying on the ground, a huge crack evident in the middle of the screen.

"I—I'm sorry," I stuttered. Suddenly, I found something interesting on the ground, the stuffed toy that was lying near my feet.

From the corner of my eyes, I saw Aiden coming closer to me. He picked up his stuffed animal from the ground and sat beside me on the soft comfortable sofa. My heart was beating faster when he placed the toy on my lap. Slowly, he closed the gap between us, and to my surprise, he landed a kiss on my forehead. I could feel something warm filling my cheeks.

Then he whispered in my ear, "You naughty childish girl. I want to be mad at you, but somehow, I just can't. What are you doing to me, Constanza?"

Carefully, I took a deep breath and swallowed once more. "I don't know," I replied him, sounding a bit afraid.

When he noticed how I tensed and froze, he broke my mood by laughing so hard that I stared at him, confused and eyes wide. I blinked. "What's funny?" I asked. "I just broke every single thing inside your office, and you're supposed to scold me so harshly until I cry!"

He brushed a tear off his eye and smiled at me. "Why would I do that, my little Stanza? There's nothing in this place that I can't replace with a blink of an eye. I can replace anything but you. But you do need to promise me not break any of my things every again."

His voice was full of command that I started thinking of what would happen to me if I decided to make the same mistake again. Nervousness seeped into my veins as his eyes searched into me. Secretly, I was thinking of making a voodoo doll of him so I could threaten him in case this thing happen the second time.

"I wonder what you're thinking about right now," he said in a sudden. "You're not planning to murder me, are you?"

"Voodoo doll," I spluttered by mistake and quickly covered my mouth with one hand. Aiden smirked, and his hand reached my cheek, making me blush obviously.

Chuckling, he winked at me. "You're so easy to read," he commented.

I pushed away his hand off me, totally annoyed. "I hate you," I said. "So how's the meeting? It's been hours."

"It's been three hours actually, and that was enough to create this headache that won't go away," he muttered. "I'm so glad I'm finally out of that dreading room. People won't cooperate that I have to use my persuading skills. In the business world, people are mean. They have no heart."

Heartless.

I gulped as I thought of that, and Aiden looked at me with a strange expression before shaking his head. "I think that's enough for tonight. Sadly, I have to take you home," he said.

I exhaled. "Okay."

He opened the door like a gentleman and let me out first before closing the door of his office. His finger pressed the elevator button, and then we were descending down my favorite radio station building. It didn't take five minutes before I was seated back on his luxurious car, heading home.

Home wasn't always heaven, but it was enough. Sure, my parents could be gone most of the time, but I was grateful that I didn't have to endure the pain Aiden had gone through. I would've died of a heart attack if I were in his position. Wondering how Aiden didn't go insane, I kept staring at the outside world as Aiden made the car accelerate.

This anthropology project changed everything, and I wouldn't have guessed that this ridiculous subject could introduce me to the One. Thinking of the possibility of this to happen was just impossible. Grinning, I was determined to make anthropology my favorite subject this year. Tomorrow, we would be handing our project, which means I have to face school that despised Aiden.

"What would happen to you tomorrow?" I asked him. "The school hates you."

He shrugged it off like it didn't matter. "They never actually liked me anyway."

"The girls are kissing your every step," I pointed out, making him roll his eyes. "I'm just stating the truth."

"If they do have a problem, I don't really care, but I'm sure they won't try to make any mess. After all, they know who I am now. They won't try to mess with the sole owner of the SKYLER group, would they?" he said, smirking. His ego was coming back, and it was my turn to roll my eyes.

"You rule the school like a shark under water. After all, you would still be on top of the food chain even with everyone's company merged together," I stated the truth. He was very rich, indeed, probably on the top of the rich guy list. I was surprised that a teenage guy could handle everything: the assets and the fame of being a pure billionaire.

"How do you even control all these assets you have?" I asked him.

His eyes shimmered as the sun began to rise, signaling us of the morning. "I'm just a pure genius. That suffices all necessary quality of a leader," he said proudly.

I gagged playfully, and he laughed. "You should be a comedian," he remarked.

"Very funny, Skyler," I mumbled. Then my mansion came into view. Before I knew it, I was saying my goodbye to Aiden. He gave me a smile, and I hugged him tightly as he planted another kiss on my cheek.

"Goodbye, Aiden. Be safe," I called before exiting his car.

"Nothing will go wrong," he quoted me as he waved a goodbye.

I could feel his pair of eyes watching my every step as I walked into the interior part of my house. And it never made sense to me why the world was so cruel. Never did I know that it would be the last time I would say goodbye to him again for a long time.

And I was serious. It was so long, almost an eternity.

An eternity with tears.

An eternity without Aiden Skyler.

"Deep trust can crush you to the bones."

"I thought you hate cars."

"They died in a car accident."

"Nothing is going to go wrong."

"Dad used to say that. But everything went wrong on the same night he said that."

One minute, I was laying my head on top of my pillow. My fingers were fiddling with the lettered buttons on my phone, and my eyes scanned down the twitter page. All the other students at school who I followed were tweeting about Aiden and their new point of view of him.

The next minute, my phone vibrated, and an unknown number was displayed on my phone. I wrinkled my forehead, wondering who was calling. A strange feeling of sadness and cautiousness flowed through me. Hesitantly, I pressed the answer button and placed the phone on my ears.

I gulped as I spelled, "H—hello?"

A hurried voice filled my eardrums, making me dreadful. "Constanza Adeline. Is this Constanza Adeline?" a man sounded from the other end of the phone line.

"Yes," I said. "Excuse me, but may I ask what's—"

"I'm Lawyer Clark," he said in a rushed tone. "And Aiden is—"

"What happened to Aiden?" I asked, worried immediately.

There was silence from the other end of the phone, and my eyes started to water when the words that came out of his mouth came down shattering my world. Memories of his embrace and his warmth filled my mind, and I let out a cry as Mr. Clark said the two words that struck my heart with pain.

"Car accident," he said.

"I'm afraid."

"We all have to face our fears, right?"

"Accidents happen everywhere."

My world was starting to blur as I pulled one of my parents' cars and rushed toward the place of accident. By the time I was there, police cars had filled the entire place. Other students from my school were already crowding the place. Rachel was there. Her eyes grew wide as an ambulance rushed out of the accident area.

Everyone around looked at me with sadness as tears started rolling down my cheek. I almost fell if Rachel didn't pull me into a tight embrace, expressing how sorry she was for judging Aiden so harshly. By then, the members of the school community had arrived in the place of accident.

An assistant of Mr. Clark decided to replace Aiden to explain what really happened to his life, making the school grow guilty and disgusted of their acts on Aiden. The assistant also mentioned how Aiden stopped believing and why he didn't want people to be too close to him. He was too damaged to trust, and he was sorry that he couldn't trust anyone anymore, that he was working his best to trust again.

Flowers surrounded the perimeter of a crashed car, and I was immobilized right across the road. Tears kept clogging my vision, but my hand refused to wipe the tears away. My mouth wouldn't do its work as people muttered their apologies to me. I didn't know how to respond and what to respond. It was all too late.

His parents died in a car crash.

Could this be the end of him too?

How can the world be this cruel?

"Stanza, look at me," Rachel said, cupping my face with her hands. "Do you want me to take you to the hospital? Do you want to meet him?"

My body managed to force a nod, and Rachel pulled me into her car. And then, we were racing with time, racing towards the hospital. My mind was in a state of shock even when Mr. Clark approached me. He shook his head. He pointed to a door at the end of a hall, a door to the surgery room. The sight of it made me grow weak, and I leaned on the wall for support, as I grew pale.

"H—how's Aiden?" my mouth managed to say out.

Like a cue, a doctor came out of the surgery room and looked at us guiltily. Words were exchanged, but I only caught a few sentences.

"—A severe injury that hurts the brain—he's in a deep sleep, a coma—"

"—Will he wake up?"

"I'm not sure, but we're trying out best—"

This heart was broken.

Is our love one sided now?

Are you still here, Aiden?

You haven't left me, have you?

I never realized that our love was bleeding since the beginning. Cracks grew from the core of our hearts, separating us. Our hard work turned in vain. Something that happened for the very first time with us fell into the ground, buried deep as time passed by.

This bleeding love.

This truth that crippled me with pain.

This eternity I have to spend without him.

Wake up, please.

I'll love you forever, wait for you to come back.

Wake up, Aiden, please.

:(I know. Accidents happen everywhere... I'm sorry for such an ending of a chapter ... peace.... Ast out for a moment ;)

Say something

Happy early Christmas to everyone :D Here's the last chapter to His Rich Highness. I can't believe it's finally the time to release my two beloved characters: Aiden and Stanza. When I look back, I remember myself planning this story on the way home from the mountain, looking at the city lights from above. It's been such a pleasure to write this story, and without all my readers' support, I know I couldn't make all this possible! Yaay! I completed my first short story :) We've made it! Thank you everyone :D I will always love you all <3

-Ast

Dedicated to another of my most favorite author! :D

Chapter 11—Say something

Christmas came to an end just by a blink of an eye. No one really cared, and in the eyes of all the other students at school, Christmas was just a passing moment to get to a new year, a new beginning. But this year, Christmas meant the world to me. It created sparks that I could never imagine happening to me, to us.

One stupid project can unite two broken hearts under the mistletoe. One moment, we're glaring at each other, and the next, we passionately tasted each other. Then, our bond shattered into pieces, just because of an accident. It came to an end by a blink of an eye, as quickly as breathing.

In a loss of words, my feet brought back to sit down inside the Anthropology classroom. Mr. Rene gave his usual speech before we all head over for winter break, and when his eyes shifted to me, those eyes softened. By this time, the whole school had known about the accident, and they've also figured out that I wasn't in a mood to talk about it. I was almost equally depressed.

"Collect your projects," Mr. Rene said. Slowly, I took the printed version of our essay out of my bag. My fingers traced his name on the front cover. I didn't know I could miss someone this much. With reasons, I long for his touch, his smile, his laugh, and his arms to wrap around me. I hoped for Aiden. I wished for Aiden Skyler.

Slowly, I got to the front of the classroom. Mr. Rene looked at me with sad eyes. "Are you done with your project, Stanza?" he asked, careful not to hurt my feelings.

I stared at him, unknowing what to answer.

He cleared his throat. "If you're not yet done, you can collect it to me anytime. I know your partner—"he coughed when he mentioned Aiden—"is not in a condition to be able to work with you. If you both want to do some modification—"

I quickly interrupted him. "We're done," I said, barely a whisper.

"Excuse me?"

"We're done," I clarified with a louder voice. With trembling hands, I gave him our report, the report we had done in a restaurant when he first kissed me. Hesitant, Mr. Rene grabbed the tip of the paper and flipped through our essay. His eyes widened when he saw the vocabularies and how neatly structured our essay way. Aiden was, as always, all about perfection.

"It's beautifully written," he said as he looked at me, his eyes full of wonders.

"Aiden structured and fixed all the mistakes. He's a good writer," I admitted.

My teacher acknowledged me with a nod before gesturing me to go and sit back down. Then everything was a blur, like watching through frosted glass. He said his greetings for us, and before I knew it, every single student in the classroom started to head out for their holiday. I saw Rachel giving me a sad smile. She nudged her head to the door, and I got up from my seat, my shoulders heavy as I followed her out.

"It's winter break," Rachel said in an attempt to cheer me up. So far, it wasn't working, and I pouted as we headed for our lockers.

To make her feel better, I nodded, although unsure what I was supposed to answer.

"What are you going to do for the break?" she questioned, but then, she realized that my answer wouldn't make me feel any better. It only reminded me of his situation now.

"Just going to the hospital, in case he wakes up."

Rachel furrowed her forehead. "Who's replacing Aiden for all his work now?"

I shrugged. "I think Lawyer Clark is working on it. We shouldn't worry about that. The real problem now is: will he ever wake up? It's been a whole week, Rachel! I'm going crazy." By this time, I was considering pulling every single strand of hair on my head.

She sighed and placed a hand on my shoulder. I shrunk and leaned on the wall for support. I've never felt this weak before, so broken and injured. "It's my first love, and I'm going to lose him. Wow, I'm living a sad fairy tale life," I complained. "It's so pathetic to hear me, I know."

Suddenly, her arms were around me, and I felt warmth travel through my body as Rachel tightened our hug. When she let go of me, I looked at her, blank. Instead of giving me a strange look, Rachel gave me a soft smile to show me that she understands my feelings now.

"Be a bit more positive, Stanza. I'm sure he'll wake up," she assured.

"How can you be so sure?" I challenged.

"Because I believe so. The whole school believes so, and you believe that too, deep inside your heart. We're all praying for him, and for the sake of his loved ones, he would never give up to stay alive," Rachel ranted on. "After all, although I loathed him, I believe Skyler is a good guy."

That caught my attention, and I started at her, eyes wide. "You finally think he's good?"

She rolled her eyes. "I thought I've apologized on everything that night."

I bowed my head. "Sorry, too distracted about the whole accident."

"What do you want to do now? Everyone's going to Richardson's party to take a break from school. You know that Richard kid? He's the heir of that car brand. I forgot what brand it is, though—"Rachel kept mumbling about the party.

"Nah, I won't got," I stopped her from her next rant.

"Why?" she asked, pretending to be shock. She knew my answer.

I smiled. "I must go to Aiden."

Before I slid into his room, I took a deep breath to calm myself. Seeing him in a deep sleep, medical machines surrounding him, made me shiver, and I wanted to break down whenever I realized he couldn't smile at me anymore. He couldn't, not now but maybe later. But we don't know the world's definition of later. Later can be tomorrow, next week, next month, in a decade, or even never.

As soon as my body adjusted to the coldness of his hospital room, I spotted Lawyer Clark sitting near his bed. He was staring at the tubes that were attached to several parts of Aiden's body and his lifeless skin. From the corner of my teary eyes, I could see scars left after the accident covering some part of his skin. Bandages were wrapped around his head.

The whole sight made me light headed, and I almost fell to the ground, hard, if I didn't spot a chair where I could land. Lawyer Clark blinked, and he greeted me a hello. My head could only nod, my eyes still focused on Aiden. It's ironic really. In some other part of the world, people could be celebrating this birthday, and in another part, others were suffering from their lost ones. On the same moment, people are laughing, and others are crying.

That's why the world is cruel and unpredictable, cold and heartless.

But somehow, we must learn to embrace it.

"Are you giving up on him?"

I was stunned, and for a moment, I was in silence. "Why do you as me that?" I questioned Mr. Clark.

He tensed before placing a hand on Aiden's immovable hand. "He can never wake up. Will you wait for him until the end of the world?" he queried.

And my answer came from the bottom of my heart. "I'll wait," I answered honestly.

Surprisingly, he laughed. "It's nice to see young love. I found it amusing and nice to watch new love bloom. This guy over here—"he pointed at Aiden—"could barely believe in the word love itself. He deleted it from his dictionary! I'm happy that he find the One."

I blushed when he mentioned the One. "I'm happy that I met him too, Sir," I admitted. "I never knew he was capable to be so gentle."

"He is amazing, a good boy with deep secrets no one could possibly understand, but somehow, you manage to understand him. Take care of him well, Miss Adeline," he managed to say. I could sense his tiredness from his voice, hoarse and dry. He must have watched for Aiden all night.

I got up from my seat. "Maybe you should take a rest, Mr. Clark. I'll take care of him here," I suggested him.

He nodded at me before heading off for the door.

Then, I was alone again with Aiden.

When I stared at his face, I couldn't help but reminisced our moments together. I stumbled and fell. He would catch me in his arms, and we would stare at each other's eyes, trying to read one another. Anywhere, he would follow me, like a lost dog finding its master. And I would do the same thing too.

"Hey," I said, sounding ashamed that I was talking to a sleeping Aiden. "Wake up soon, okay? Say something to me if you're ready to wake up. Then maybe we can have fun again."

I held his hand and squeezed it. "Promise me?" I whispered.

I could have sworn I felt his hand squeeze mines.

It's been a month now.

A month without the sound of his voice whispering annoying things into my ears.

Sometimes I missed his voice, his teasing, and how he told me I was too childish for my own good. I wanted to hear him just one more time. Being in his embrace and destroying his office became the highlight of my past, and I would do anything to go back in time. Another time, I dream to teleport myself back to the past. Maybe then I could stop him from driving a car. Then he wouldn't be in this situation.

He wanted to embrace his fears, but his fears came back, drowning him in the same pool.

When I glanced out through the window, I could see how the snow-covered ground was starting to melt. I sensed spots of greens, indicating the emerging new plants coming for the summer. My eyes were wide when I saw the trees shaking off the snow on its branches, hitting on the pedestrians walking by. Secretly, I laughed when a pile of snow landed on a dog's face, but then, the sound of a beeping machine brought me back to reality.

I looked back to his bed where Aiden was lying immobilized for days. They say people who got into coma were actually flying around the world, searching for something that went missing in their life. And now, I wondered if Aiden was circling around the world, searching for a missing piece of him. Or maybe his spirit could be in this hospital room, staring at me as I stared at his human form.

Suddenly, my phone buzzed under my jeans. When I looked at the screen, I saw Rachel's number appear in green. My finger pressed the answer button and brought the phone to my ear.

"The number you are calling—" I tried to imitate the operator guy.

"Shut up, Stanza. I know you're there," she retorted.

I grinned. "Sorry, but what do you want?"

"Turn on TalkMusic, now," she said in a hurry, and before I could say another thing, she ended our call, leaving me in a daze. My curiosity took over, and I turned to the radio Mr. Clark had brought to the hospital the other day to keep me entertained.

Welcome back to TalkMusic! Winter is almost over, people, and before you know it, we're going to face one blazing summer year! Hell, yeah, isn't it exciting? To keep you comfortable, here's a song to keep you awake! This song can also calm the hearts that are losing someone, probably a broken heart from a broken love. Here's Say Something.

Then the sad music filled my ears. Deep inside, I know every single lyric could relate to me, to this broken heart buried deep inside.

Anywhere I would've followed you.

Say something I'm giving up on you.

And I swallow my pride.

You're the one that I love.

And I'm saying goodbye.

I shook my head. This wasn't goodbye. I looked over at Aiden. "Are you ready to say something?" I asked him. "I don't think this is goodbye. I hope you think the same thing as I do."

Now, I wondered if a miracle could happen.

His eyes twitched.

I blinked. "Aiden?"

His fingers started moving.

"Hello?" I knew it was a dumb question to ask. Squeezing his hand, I let the music fill my ears.

Slowly, he squeezed back my hand.

I gasped when his eyelashes fluttered.

Then his eyes were opened. His gaze landed on me, a shock was clearly shown on his face. I waited for him to process everything. He looked at the hospital walls and the tubes surrounding him. I caught him wince when he examined his injuries that almost healed.

"Hello, Aiden," I said.

He looked at me.

"Do you remember me?" I asked.

A smile crawled into his face.

"Yes, Stanza. I remember you."

I smiled. "Welcome back."

His Rich Highness is back.

The End

You have just read 23400 words :) Congratulations!

Announcements of new book in the "Simplicity Series"

Hello there readers of His Rich Highness :) I have an announcement to make. I've decided to make a series based on short stories, and I'm going to name it the "Simplicity" Series. The simplicity series is about the fragility of life, how it's important to embrace who you really are. There's going to be three short stories in the "Simplicity" Series.

Book 1: His Rich Highness

Aiden and Stanza showed us how fragile life was. Love blossoms in one second, and in another, it can be taken away by just an accident.

Book 2: The Boy Who Forgets

Alex zoned from being popular to barely visible at school. And now, Valerie is going to find out what's wrong about him. "I try to be grateful in sadness, pain, and misery," he said.

Book 3: (untitled) Coming soon

Anyway, the message is basically this:

If you like HIS RICH HIGHNESS, we're going to be seeing a bit of Stanza and AIden in "The Boy Who Forgets". But now, we have a similar simple love line with sadness by Alex and Valerie. If you like His Rich Highness, "The Boy Who Forgets" is very recommended. :D Please, readers of His Rich Highness, let's enter the second book of the Simplicity Series, the sequel to His Rich Highness: The Boy Who Forgets. Link below :)

CPSIA information can be obtained
at www.ICGtesting.com
Printed in the USA
LVHW040252020323
740706LV00017B/1658

9 781805 096610